HARD WORK

USA TODAY BESTSELLING

BLAIR BABYLON

Here's the problem: when Caz is injured in a suspicious car accident, the hospital won't let him go home alone. While under the influence of controlled substances, he begs his friend, his work wife, the secret love of his life, to stay in his mansion with him until he's back on his feet.

He knew her three ragamuffin cats were part of the bargain.

But she's married to a guy who treats her like dirt, who doesn't appreciate her, and who was doing something asinine in Bali when Rox got thrown out of her apartment and needed rescuing.

But now Caz is injured, vulnerable, and he just loves watching television with her at night.

And when she pokes him in the ribs and it turns into tickle, which turns into a tussle, which turns into something he hadn't intended, he doesn't know what to do.

Not letting your co-worker know you've fallen in love with her is Hard Work.

PRAISE FOR BLAIR BABYLON

PRAISE FOR BILLIONAIRES IN DISGUISE: MAXENCE

"Maxence is everything I love in a romance novel - a whipsmart man with an anguishing call to serve that conflicts with his love for Dree. I was spellbound!" - New York Times bestselling author Julia Kent

"What a wild and sexy race through Paris! Rogue masterfully combines nail biting suspense with high steam for the ride of your life with Maxence and Dree." ~ USA Today bestselling author JJ Knight

"**Another masterpiece from Blair Babylon, who I am convinced keeps getting better and better.** Max is not at all as I'd imagined him, and really it's no wonder, since he has been forced to repress who he is. The real Max keeps popping up his head, doing real-Max things that the other Max wishes he wouldn't do. He struggles with his inner demons to be a Godly man, but he hasn't quite figured out how to balance the different parts of himself, and as a result, tortures himself. He is a man searching for himself, impeded by too many bad guys who wish him harm. It's hard to focus on self-actualization while trying to simply survive without getting yourself killed." -- E.C., Goodreads Reviewer

"Blair's stories have always been hot but this one might be the hottest yet." -- Xtreme Delusions Book Blog

"I just couldn't stop reading! This book is addictive!" -- Kat, Goodreads Reviewer

"Rogue is a phenomenal romantic suspense that is sure to delight and entertain as it holds your heart and mind captive. Nothing can prepare you for the roller coaster ride that is Maxence. He will take you unawares and leave you completely breathless and wanting. If nothing else, you will learn why he is so addicting to the women that he meets." -- Words Are The Breath of Life Book Blog

"Good gosh! Author Blair Babylon is a master at building suspense. I have been eagerly awaiting Maxence's story for YEARS. Finally it arrives and I am practically salivating as I tear into the book, excited that I will finally learn the truth about the elusive Maxence. As I am reading, I am finding that Maxence's unveiling is happening at the rate of an excruciatingly slow strips tease. The end of "Rogue" finds me with almost as many questions regarding who Maxence is as the beginning of the book-- but I promise that slooowly he is starting to be unveiled. **One thing that is made abundantly clear is that Maxence lives two polar opposite lives and this results in my finding myself even MORE intrigued by him. Now**

THIS is what I consider phenomenal writing!" -- Lil Miss Reads A Lot Book Blog

PRAISE FOR EVERY BREATH YOU TAKE

"The book oozed heart and passion from every page, it was as if it was traveling through my fingers to touch my very soul - I'm gobsmacked at how I feel about it! It showed more than I thought I was going to get it gave me *love and passion in absolute bin loads and moreover it was full of desire, hope, longing, honesty and devotion* - not just from the characters but from the author also because her devotion to her craft was clearly evident in this book - she nailed it!!" -- *Books Laid Bare Blog, (Every Breath You Take, Rock Stars in Disguise: Xan)*

"*Every Breath You Take* was an absolutely stunning and creatively passionate exploration of two lost and lonely people finding the missing part of their heart and soul in each other. What a breathtaking journey filled with unwanted hope, unwavering love, and unexpected devotion! This series is continuing with such a brilliant depth of heart and soul that I just can't get enough of. I am definitely looking forward to more of these ground-breaking stories." --*Shadowplay Book Blog, (Every Breath You Take, Rock Stars in Disguise: Xan)*

"The writing is great, as usual, and the characters are so well developed. **Author Blair Babylon has extreme talent here."** -- *Sammy's Book Obses-*

sion Blog, (Every Breath You Take, Rock Stars in Disguise: Xan)

"This book brings together two of the author's series, Billionaires in Disguise and Rock Stars in Disguise. Prior to this book, the two were entirely separate. If you haven't yet read any of the books in these series, then what are you waiting for? **You do not need to read them to understand this book, but reading them will give you a broader understanding of the incredible canvas Blair is using as her background. She has basically created these worlds and characters from scratch, and what a world it is."** *~Fictional Men's Page for Book Ho's*

"**This was one incredible story.** I can't wait to continue with this series." *~Books and Beyond Fifty Shades*

"Let me first say WOW... I am seriously addicted to Blair Babylon's books her imagination whether it be Crime, Rockstar or Billionaire. **She creates a world where you are immersed with colourful and diverse characters and situations that you don't want to escape from."** *~Kat's Book Promotions*

PRAISE FOR BLAIR BABYLON'S BOOKS

"What a pair! This story had me clutching my chest. **I loved Tryp. His damaged and broken soul tugs at your heart strings.** His need to spiral down into the darkness to escape his past will have you wanting to comfort him and just whisper sweet nothings in his ear. The unlikely friendship was definitely the perfect route for this story. It takes a special kind of person to handle all of Tryp's darkness. Elfie definitely proved herself worthy and I loved her determination and strength even though she has a past of her own that she is desperately trying to run from. **Blair Babylon delivers a truly emotional story that had me on one helluva emotional rollercoaster.** I am definitely looking forward to reading more from this series." *~Jennifer's Book Obsession, (Somebody to Love, Rock Stars in Disguise: Tyrp)*

"Just believe me when I say you DON'T want to miss this one." *~Jo's Book Addictions (Somebody to Love, Rock Stars in Disguise: Tyrp)*

"This was my first Blair Babylon book and I was on a rollercoaster. **Tryp and Elfie need to read by all, a raw story of friendship and love.** Truly only the strong survive. I want more of these two."*~Romance Bytes (Every Breath You Take, Rock Stars in Disguise: Xan)*

"The chemistry Wulf and Raegan have is amazing and the fact that they are both so stubborn makes their relationship funny at times. The series covers everything from finding out about the good, bad, and ugly of each other to meeting the family. There are raw emotions in these books." *~~Random Musesomy Book Blog*

"Blair Babylon knows what she is doing. **This is some of the best romance I have read,**

hands down. It's got a little bit of everything, for everyone....the story was so well written, infused with sex, humor and drama, that **I would gladly read it over and over again."** ~*Contagious Reads Blog*

"If I could give 10 stars I would! I adore this book, I have read it two times completely and many times parts of it." ~*Katrina's Books Blog*

"AWESOME! When I first started reading this book I thought it was going to be your regular romance book and I thought, what kind of spin could possibly be put on this kind of relationship. Don't get me wrong, I am the first person to admit that I love a good relationship. I think it's hot but I was still waiting for a new refreshing spin on romance novels, and this was it for me. So of course you still had the typical kind of damsel in distress and then that sexy as hell man coming to save her. **Well the twist is something that you wouldn't expect....** Wulf also has a secret, and when I mean secret, it's a big secret. No, it's nothing that you might be thinking, like he is married or he is gay. **I mean huge, I was in complete shock when I found out.** That is one of the things that I loved most about this novel, **everything that I thought was completely wrong and it kept me intrigued the entire time.**" ~*Fictional Book Ho's Blog*

"The writing was great and author, Blair Babylon, has an impeccable vocabulary! I loved that she uses so many less commonly used words. Her characters are extensively developed and **I loved**

the way the author "peeled away" the layers of them and let us really get to know them gradually. I loved the mystery in the characters backgrounds and personalities. **I loved the suspense and action thrown in the story also!"** ~*Sammy's Book Obsession*

HARD WORK

SECRET BILLIONAIRES

CASIMIR

USA TODAY BESTSELLING AUTHOR

BLAIR BABYLON

MALACHITE PUBLISHING LLC

This is a work of fiction.
Names, characters, places and incidents are either products of the author's wild and naughty imagination or are used fictitiously. Any resemblance to actual events or locales or persons, living or dead, is entirely coincidental.

1st Edition: May, 2016

Created with Vellum

CONTENTS

HARD WORK

SECRET BILLIONAIRES

CASIMIR

USA TODAY BESTSELLING AUTHOR

BLAIR BABYLON

AMSBERG V. ARBEITMAN

Outside the door of the conference room where the DiCaprio people were waiting, Rox paused just in case Cash needed a pep talk or to process what she had said and damn well meant, but he smiled at her while he held the door for her, just like normal. They walked in together, wearing their bitch faces.

Inside, senior partner Valerie Arbeitman was already sitting at the conference table, a tablet and notepad in front of her.

Valerie asked, "What are you two doing here?"

Rox stopped, and Cash stiffened beside her. "We're here for the contract discussion. What are you doing here?"

"When you weren't back from your car accident, I took my clients back."

"This case was shuffled to us when you had your stroke."

"You didn't call in to say that you were coming back today, anyway."

"Rox notified people, and I haven't missed a meeting."

Rox nodded, confirming that she had notified them. Rox never missed confirming meetings. Missed meetings were horrendously expensive.

Cash said, "I've teleconferenced or moved them, but I've never left people waiting. We've prepared for this meeting for weeks. We're ready."

"I'm ready," Val said.

"Are you?" Cash's voice dropped. "Are you ready to explain what *all* of the clauses mean, even Section Twelve point Six?"

Rox stared at the computer in her arms. That section dealt with DiCaprio's compensation, and the studio had slipped in that he would get a percentage of the *net* profits from the film, where they had already negotiated for the *gross* profits. With all the deductions and depreciations that studios can claim, movies never, ever make *net* profits. They were trying to screw him out of millions with that one word.

"Of course," Valerie said, her magenta lips pursing.

Cash turned to the legal team sitting on the other side of the table. "Is it on the agenda?"

The lawyer in the middle picked up a piece of paper. Not a brown hair on her sleek, short hair waved as she bent and examined the paper. "No. It's not."

"The studio changed his compensation to *net* profits," Cash said.

The other lawyers gasped and bobbled in their chairs. Rox tried not to smile at their reaction.

"You still want her to advise you?" Cash asked them.

They fidgeted. Rox stepped back and grabbed the door's handle.

"We could hold the meeting with both of you," the lawyer in the middle said.

Valerie stood and swept her tablet and paper into her hands. "You take this meeting. I'll see you later."

Rox opened the door for her. Valerie's hands were full, and it seemed like a slight courtesy to allow her to save some face.

Cash leaned toward Valerie as she passed him. "We've read all your contracts. There are a lot of clauses you have missed that we need to discuss."

Valerie stalked out, silent rage pouring out of her.

He smiled at the lawyers on the other side of the table. "Ladies, may I present my associate, Roxanne Neil. We may now proceed with the meeting."

Cash pulled out a chair for Rox, as usual. She sat and handed out the agenda.

"Net profits?" the lead lawyer asked Rox.

"Oh, yes," Rox told her, "and there's a lot more than that to discuss."

Chapter Fifty-Two

THREE YEARS

Rox stood in her office, leaning on her desk and breathing after finishing the DiCaprio meeting.

The three ashen-faced lawyers had left the conference room quickly after the meeting wrapped up and didn't even glance at Valerie's closed office door as they hurried through the office.

Rox had fled, too. After her temper tantrum with Cash before the meeting, she hadn't wanted to deal with him.

They had never had a fight with each other in the three years that they had been working together. Sure, they mutually and cooperatively shouted about contracts. That was part of the scene and the game.

But actually fight with each other? They hadn't had to. Nothing mattered enough. They were just colleagues and buddies.

He had never been able to hurt her before.

Rox wished her cats were hiding under her desk.

Cuddling something furry would be calming right now.

A knock rattled her door. Cash peeked through the window that cut the wall beside the door. His chin was lowered, and his green eyes serious.

Rox nodded to him.

He opened the door and leaned into her office. "Can we talk?"

"Yeah. Come on in."

He stepped through her door and closed it behind himself. "You were right. You belonged in that meeting."

She nodded. "This is weird. I don't like fighting with you."

"I don't like it either."

"So let's stop. Let's just, don't."

He nodded and walked around her desk. "You were right about another thing, too. You are my paralegal first. I need you to work with me. Whatever happens, I don't want you to resign your position."

"I don't want to quit. I love my job. Are we going to be able to travel together after this?"

"We've been friends for three years. Surely, we can figure it out." He looked down, staring at his shoes. "Is this just a superficial affair for you?"

"It never is, with me. And it sure isn't now, especially because it's *you.* That's why I made up the whole Grant thing. I've always known that I'm the one who's going to end up with a broken heart."

"But what if you don't?" he asked.

"Right. Maybe I won't." Her flat voice sounded sarcastic, which she hadn't meant. She couldn't even look up from her hands.

Soft footsteps padded on the carpet. He stood beside her, and he lifted her hand off the desk and held it in his warm, strong fingers. She let him hold onto her hand, but she still couldn't look at him. Foreboding ran through her, darkening every outcome she could think of.

Cash lifted her hand. His soft lips just brushed her fingertips. He said, "Maybe I'll be the one with a broken heart."

Her gulping laugh sounded more like a sob, and she covered her mouth with her other hand.

He wrapped his arms around her and pressed her to him. "No matter what happens, we will be friends afterward. You can't go through all the things that we have together and not remain friends. You've helped me escape from the Russian prostitute delivered to my room, and I've cock-blocked Italians with eight hands who were accosting you. We'll always have that, and we had that first. I owe you greatly for getting us out of that traffic situation in Argentina."

"I just unbuttoned my blouse a little and flirted with the soldier," she demurred.

"I would probably still be in prison down there."

"Yeah, and I've heard that their prisons suck. They don't even have WiFi."

"Indeed. And that time in Egypt, when you wore hijab and sneaked in to talk to opposing counsel's mother and told her that she could meet Harrison Ford if the deal went through? We would have never finished that negotiation without her demanding that her son arrange for her to meet Harrison."

"Yeah, that was fun. She was so excited when she was on the set that day."

"And that other time when we were in New Jersey and took a wrong turn in Camden."

"You wanted to pull over and ask somebody for directions because we couldn't get a cell phone signal to use the GPS. Those guys were drug dealers. You're so naive."

He stroked her hair. "I think I owe my life to you on more than one occasion. That time in Hong Kong?"

"I had to undo *three* buttons to get you away from those guys. Maybe Arthur was right and you do need security."

He chuckled, and his deep laugh reverberated through his chest under her cheek. "We will always be friends, and I need you as my paralegal. Are we clear?"

"Yeah," she said, and she felt a little stupid. "You probably would actually die without me to bail you out of trouble."

He stroked her hair and down her back to her waist, and his arms tightened around her. "I think I would."

Chapter Fifty-Three

AMSBERG V. ARBEITMAN, ROUND TWO

HARD WORK

CASIMIR

BLAIR BABYLON

Casimir leaned against the closed door to his office, his arms crossed tightly over his chest. The afternoon sun was dipping toward the western horizon near the corner of the windows, and the glass darkened to compensate for the glare.

This wasn't how it was supposed to happen.

When Rox finally left Grant—or whatever the hell had happened when Grant had ceased to exist—Casimir was supposed to swoop in and make Rox smile again. He was supposed to show her the wonderful life that she could have with a man who valued her. They were supposed to travel and have adventures and laugh together.

She had laughed all the time when they were just office colleagues.

She wasn't supposed to cry.

Rox was right about one thing, though. He had said many of those things to other girls. Not all of them, but many.

He had known Rox for three long years. All during that time, she had given him no sign that she would ever leave Grant, Casimir's fictional competition, so Casimir had indulged in affair after affair, waiting. None of the other women had satisfied him, each more superficial than the last, none of them as smart or reliable or personable or sensible as Rox—or as beautiful—and no matter how much he had tried to invest himself into each relationship, the time came in each affair when he just couldn't pretend any longer.

Every time, when he had realized that each woman was not and would never be Roxanne, the guilt had overwhelmed him.

That was when, as Rox had said, he had *ghosted* them.

When he took a deep breath, he could still smell her perfume on his skin.

Casimir walked to his desk. A notepad with his own handwriting—odd and with violent vertical slashes, he had been told—lay on top of his myriad other papers. The name *Valerie Arbeitman* was written across the top.

His meeting with Valerie was due to start in five minutes.

He must focus on that. He must forget this insanity concerning Rox and concentrate on this meeting with Valerie.

Much hinged on his meeting with Valerie.

Her side of the story.

The state ethics panel.

Possible criminal prosecutions.

He wished that Rox could attend the meeting with him, but if it went very, very badly, he didn't want her to lose her job, too.

He picked up the notepad and, setting his jaw, walked through the cubicle maze to the senior partners' offices.

Valerie was waiting for him at her door. "I'm glad to see that you're back and you're all right," she said. "I don't think I said that, earlier."

"And I'm glad to see that you've made a full recovery," he said.

She shrugged. "Nearly. My left side is a little weak, and my cheek feels weird." She pushed at the side of her face.

"No one could ever tell," he said, keeping his voice low.

Valerie's smile was rueful, perhaps even angry. "Always the gentleman, aren't you?"

"I try."

They walked inside Val's office, and she kicked the door shut behind them. "And yet you requested this meeting to discuss my incompetence."

Valerie was a senior partner, and she and Josie could agree to buy him out of the partnership and kick his butt to the curb with a memo. "I said that there were irregularities in your contracts that we needed to discuss, such as the net profits rather than the gross profits for DiCaprio this afternoon."

Valerie brushed her hand in the air as if their client being potentially swindled out of millions of dollars didn't matter to her. "We would have caught it on the next draft."

"There isn't supposed to be a next draft. Who did you have working on it?"

"Wren Sishi."

Casimir shook his head. Wren was stellar. She wouldn't have missed that. "I'll ask her about it. You know that she saves all her drafts."

"You're implying that I'm lying."

"While I was recovering from the car accident, I looked over many contracts from this law office. I found many irregularities in every contract that you had final approval on. *Many.* It seems that you were acting contrary to our clients' interests."

"I'm not acting contrary to their interests. I'm doing the best that I can for *everyone's* interests."

"The current rules for professional conduct don't allow you to advocate for *everyone's* interests. Just *our clients'* interests. You cannot act contrary to those. Anything else is unethical."

"It's important that I act in everyone's best interests. When I say *everyone,* I mean me, and Josie, and our associates, and you."

"This is not in *my* best interest, I assure you. I would never condone betraying even one of our clients."

Valerie leaned on her desk and stared straight at him. "Just because you don't know why doesn't mean that I'm wrong, and I am absolutely right on this. I'm the senior partner, and you need to back off."

"I won't," he said.

"I heard that you and Rox wouldn't back off when you headed into the Watson negotiation with Monty Evans. I heard *all* about it."

"We're supposed to advocate for our clients. We must act on their behalf and do our best for them."

"I can't tell you everything, Cash. You'll just have to trust me and stop pushing people."

"I can't trust you if you betray our clients."

"You need to stop pushing people now. It's getting dangerous. You were almost killed."

"That was an accident. It has nothing to do with it."

"Of course, it was an accident. You need to stop pushing people."

"Tell me why."

"Hell, no."

"You have betrayed so many of our clients. How could I trust a word you say?"

Casimir stopped, and a tremor started in his hands. He played that back in his head. *You have betrayed so many of our clients. How could I trust a word you say?*

He shook it off. This meeting was paramount.

Valerie said, "As senior partner, I'm telling you to back off. You will stop reviewing any contract that is not for one of your own clients. I don't want to hear another damn word about any of this, and you won't talk to Monty Evans again. Do you hear me?"

He stood. "You haven't heard the last of this, Valerie."

"For your sake, for all our sakes, and for the sake of this firm, I hope you'll change your mind." She looked straight at him, her brown eyes wide. "And for the love of God, if you are going to challenge Monty Evans again, leave Rox Neil out of it."

"Rox is my paralegal. She goes into all meetings with me."

"You're fucking her."

"She's my paralegal first and foremost. She's a professional woman, and I respect her."

"I am telling you, if you feel the need to go tilting at windmills again, leave her in the office."

"I'm not tilting at windmills. These are unethical actions. These contracts would swindle our clients."

"Oh, that's just your opinion."

"I assure you that it's fact."

"Take the rest of the day off. You're overwrought from coming into the office so soon after your accident."

"I am not," he growled.

"I have another appointment. Thank you for stopping by." She picked up some papers from her desk and pointedly began reading them. "And be careful driving home, Cash."

"Thank you for your time," Casimir said, measuring out his words.

He strolled through the office, smiling and talking to people while his mind whirled.

Valerie Arbeitman was lying to him about everything.

Chapter Fifty-Four

HIS HOLINESS POPE FUCKITALL

HARD WORK

CASIMIR

2

BLAIR BABYLON

After Cash had untangled himself and left her office, citing that he needed to talk to someone, Rox swallowed hard to dispel any remaining heebee-jeebees and was holding her cell phone to her ear while it rang, calling Cash's house phone.

A man answered, "Casimir van Amsberg's residence. Good afternoon, Roxanne."

Arthur's rich baritone didn't even sound sleepy, and his British accent was as sharp as cut crystal.

She said, "Hey, Arthur. I was seeing if Maxence was up?" Because she had assumed that Arthur would be sleeping off his drunk for hours yet.

"Oh, no. His Holiness Pope Fuckitall is still asleep."

"You sound, um, *okay?*"

"Of course. Slept it off like a champ, as usual."

"That's impressive," she said.

"I deeply appreciate the water and salts this morning. That helped a lot."

"If I had been that wasted, I would have needed an I.V. and an exorcist."

Arthur laughed. "How is our lad doing on his first day back at work?"

"Fine. He's alpha-maling everyone else in the office, as usual."

"He's going after other women?" Arthur sounded confused.

"Oh, no. He's just reestablishing his place in the pecking order. He's already challenged two other guys to a game of basketball on the parking structure's roof after work. Do you and Maxence want to meet us for a late supper?"

"He's challenged *two* blokes? Does he play two-on-one?"

"Oh, no. He and Draven play two-on-two against the other guys."

"Tell Draven to switch teams. I'll roust Sleeping Moody out of bed, and we'll play three-on-three, just like old times."

"Okay. I'll tell him."

And then she would tell all the women in the office to get their butts up to the roof.

This was going to be *epic.*

Chapter Fifty-Five
FUN AND GAMES

Oh, and it was.

Rox and the other women and a few of the gay men stood around the makeshift basketball court and watched the glorious display of manflesh in the setting sun.

Because all that is holy was smiling that day, Cash lost the coin toss, and so Cash, Arthur, and Maxence were the "skins" team.

As the three men stripped off their shirts, revealing rippling muscle stacked upon rippling muscle, Rox thought that several of the women in the audience were close to having seizures.

Cash and the other guys played hard, sweat glistening on their bodies. Tattoos flashed. The ball slammed into the asphalt and through hands and swished down the hoops as the men turned and jumped, blocking and ducking, for an hour.

Every striation of muscle was visible on Maxence. He had truly burned down to zero percent body fat. Maybe he still had a few cells' worth far deep inside, but none was showing.

The onlookers were relatively sure that Cash and his guys won the game, but the scorekeeper got distracted and lost count twice, so no one really knew for sure.

And no one cared.

Rox was distracted as heck because every time that Cash, Maxence, or Arthur raised their hands over their heads to shoot, she could see the matching tattoo that they all had on the insides of their right arms: three shields joined at the tops around a Celtic knot.

She had to corner Cash and ask about that.

And other things. *Man.*

Afterward, Cash, Arthur, and Maxence went to Cash's gym around the corner to shower, and Rox waited at the office for them to come back so they could go out to supper.

About fifteen minutes later, Rox spotted Wren walking back to her cubicle, and she herded Wren into the ladies' room, whispering, "I need to talk to you."

"I can't believe you guys kicked Valerie Arbeitman out of a meeting," Wren whispered and started to reapply her cherry lip gloss. "She fumed all the way to her office and slammed the door."

"I need to ask you about Cash," Rox said.

"Oh?" Wren's gaze turned wary.

"When you were going out with Cash—"

"Why?" Wren asked, holding her lip gloss aside.

"Just a question. No reason."

"Are you involved with him?"

"Maybe a little," Rox admitted.

Wren dropped her lip gloss and scrambled to grab it before it dropped off the counter. "But you're married!"

"I'm actually not. I kind of made that whole thing up."

"What do you mean, *kind of* made that whole thing up?"

Wren was a damn good paralegal. Rox should have known that she would define the terms before anything else. "It means that I totally made Grant up. The pictures are headshots from a friend of mine who's an agent. The vacation pics were photoshopped. I'm not married. I've never been married. Grant doesn't exist."

"But I met him!" Wren exclaimed.

"No, you didn't."

"I did! At the barbecue last summer!"

"Nope. Must have been someone else." Rox had never brought a date to anything.

"I met him, and he told me about auditioning for something."

"Yeah, that could have been anyone in California."

"I could swear that I met him," Wren said, her long, blond hair swishing as she shook her head.

"I guarantee you didn't. I've never brought any guys to any events because Grant doesn't exist."

"Huh. I wonder who I met, then. Maybe Brochelle's fiancé."

"Yeah, maybe. Look, about Cash—"

"I can't believe that you're finally having your fling with him. We all thought that you were immune or something." She batted her eyelashes at herself, checking for mascara flakes. "Well, we all thought you were married."

"Did he ever call you anything while you guys were going out? Like a pet name?"

Wren frowned. "Like what?"

Like *lieveke.* "I don't know, like sweetheart or honey? Or something in Dutch?"

Wren's frown slipped to the side, uncomprehending. "Why would he call anybody something in Dutch?"

"Or whatever? Something British or German or something?"

Wren's gaze rose toward the white stripes of the ceiling lights. "I don't think so. How come?"

"He's—" Rox searched her own eyes in the mirror. Her eyes looked afraid, overly large and dirt brown. "It seems like he's coming on strong."

"Is he pressuring you to do things that you don't want to?" Wren asked, her hand moving across the counter to touch Rox's wrist.

"No, no. Not like that."

"Yeah, he doesn't *have* to pressure anyone," she smirked.

"Did he make you believe that he was in love with you? Is that why everyone walks around all mopey and with a broken heart afterward?"

"He never did anything like that," Wren mused. "He never said that he loved me, that's for sure, and I've never heard anyone else talk about love with him, either. He's not a lovey-dovey duck, you know? He never talks about himself. Never told me anything about his childhood or growing up in London or what England was like."

Evidently, Cash had never told her that he was Dutch.

"We never went out with anyone else, either. It was always just him and me, and it was more intense that way."

"So you never met his friends or anything."

"Oh, Lord, no. We always went to hotels. Who were those guys, playing basketball with him?"

"Just some guys he knows. So you never went back to his house?"

"No. Never his house. But we didn't hang out much in L.A., either. Either we flew somewhere or he drove us somewhere. I have a theory that he doesn't even have a house, that he spends all his salary on that car, his clothes, and dates."

Oh, that wasn't true, either.

"If anything," Wren continued, "I was very conscious the whole time that it was just fun and games, and nothing that intense and shallow could last very long. He's like a laser that way, intense light, but it only touches the surface and bounces off anything hard, and it has no mass, no gravity."

Rox curled her hands into fists. "Then why is everyone so miserable when he ghosts on them?"

"He's like catnip, you know? He's fun and a little freaky, and you have a great time laughing with him. Hanging out with him is *wild.* I never got into the office before ten-thirty. Sometimes eleven. It does feel like a game when you're with him. Not a winner-loser type of game. A non-zero-sum game where you both win, but it's definitely a game. And the dates! I didn't even have a passport when we started dating, and he got one expedited for me so we could go see a symphony in Milan that first weekend. And it was fashion week there, too, so he bought me a bunch of clothes."

"So, that's it? It's just that he buys girls a bunch of stuff and takes them on expensive dates?"

"It's more like getting on a roller coaster for a couple of weeks or months. When you get off, your legs feel funny for a while, and you want to ride it again because you were laughing and screaming the whole time."

"So you just liked riding him."

Wren laughed. "Yeah, there was that, too. He's a fun ride."

Rox flinched.

"I'm sorry. I don't mean to talk about him like that to you. While you're in the moment, it's a rush, and you should enjoy the game while it lasts."

She bit her lower lip. "What did he do before he ghosted on you? How did you know that he was going to?"

Wren glanced at her from the sides of her dark eyes. Her voice tightened. "I didn't. He blindsided me. He blindsides everyone, every time. He just closes up."

"But he must have given you some clue. There must have been something," Rox insisted.

"Nope." Wren fluffed her blond curls.

"He didn't meet someone else? He didn't start getting mysterious texts or phone calls or have other places that he had to go?"

"Not at all. I don't think he had anyone else lined up. Everything was light and laughter, and then he was gone. It was like any other day, until it wasn't."

"Yeah," Rox said, staring at her own brown, haunted eyes in the mirror. "It's always like that, just like any other day, and then they're gone."

Chapter Fifty-Six

EUROTRASH

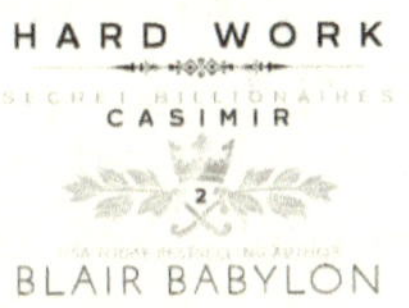

After Rox and Cash abused Maxence and Arthur with nuclear-hot Thai food during an early supper, they sat around the table, and Arthur announced that he and Maxence were catching a cab for the airport and they would be back in the morning.

"How come?" Rox asked before she saw Cash waving her off. "Not that it matters. You're big boys. You don't have to report to me."

Arthur laughed. "Did you warn her, Caz?"

Cash glared at him. "Warn her of what?"

Arthur laughed again.

Maxence, however, was staring at his empty plate and rearranging his used silverware slanted across it, not making any eye contact.

Okay, they were obviously up to something truly sordid.

Sometimes, Rox was not a nice person. "So, are you going, too, *Maxence?*"

He looked up, his dark eyes wary. "Someone has to make sure Arthur isn't face-down in a gutter after he's been in his cups."

Cash snorted something that almost sounded like a laugh.

"Someone has to take care of him. You know how he is," he told Cash.

Cash said, "You could send one of your minders with him. They're still holed up at the airport, right?"

Maxence pursed his full lips. "They won't leave me here. If I want them to go, then I have to."

Rox said, "That's right charitable of you."

Maxence glanced at her out of the corner of his eyes, a sexy squint, like he was unsure whether he was being made fun of.

Arthur clapped him on the shoulder. "Yes, Maxence. That's 'right charitable' of you, walking through Hell itself to ensure that I don't end up face-down in a puddle of my own vomit at The Devilhouse."

Now Rox suspected that she was being made fun of.

Maxence's black eyebrows pinched together, and he frowned. "I'm not a priest yet."

Arthur cracked up and pounded him on the shoulder. "That's the spirit, Maxence. And with my steadying influence and a little luck, you never will be."

Cash's voice dropped in a warning. *"Arthur."*

Maxence shook his head, his black hair falling

over his forehead. His dark eyes creased in pain. "You're right. I shouldn't go. That den of iniquity—"

"Oh, come now. It isn't that bad!" Arthur insisted.

"—is a symbol of everything that I should leave behind. The decadence. Using people as pawns and playthings. We should be better than that."

Arthur grabbed his chest. "Maxence, you'll hurt my feelings if you keep this up."

"I'm sorry, Arthur—"

"I'm fucking with you. I drowned all my feelings in thirty-year-old scotch years ago. I think you might have been there, but you were probably engaged in something worse than I was, considering those years."

Rox leaned back in her chair, unsure whose side she should be arguing for. Cash caught her eye, and even though he was wearing his blank court face, Rox could see that he was upset.

Maxence said, "Let's not go, Arthur. Surely, we can resist this temptation."

"Oh, I succumb to temptation every chance that it is offered. I'm going."

Maxence glanced at Cash. "You could go with him."

Cash shook his head. "I'm not going to The Devilhouse."

"It's Monday night," Rox piped up. "We have to go to the office tomorrow."

Cash looked down at his plate as if she had said

something gauche. Well, to heck with him. She was a hard-working Southern girl and wasn't going to crawl into the office reeking of liquor.

"We'll be back in time for work tomorrow," Arthur said. "It's only an hour flight, if that. We could be back in plenty of time to shower and get to 'work' by ten."

She could hear his quotation marks around the word 'work' as if that were an unfamiliar concept to him. Yeah, Rox just bet that it was. "Office opens at nine. Not ten."

"We could have the pilot flap those wings faster. However, if you do not have the tolerance to handle even a drink or two and function at your office the next day, perhaps it would be better to leave you three here. Such an adventure might be too rigorous for you."

Heat filled Rox's head. "I assure you, we Southern girls can hold our liquor as well as any effete Eurotrash."

"Did you hear that, Caz?" Arthur backhanded Cash on his arm. "We're Eurotrash."

"*You* are," Cash muttered. "Rox, I don't think—"

Rox continued, getting louder, "We Southerners are bottle-fed Maker's Mark until we're weaned onto Jim Beam Devil's Cut. I assure you, I am up to whatever ruckus you boys *think* you can get up to."

Arthur smiled a slow, devilish grin. "Then it's settled. We'll all go. I'll have the pilot ready the plane."

"We're not staying all night," Rox said, her voice

firm. "We're staying for three hours and flying home at midnight. You boys are barely paper-trained. Can't have you running around a strange city all hours of the night."

Arthur's malevolent grin hadn't changed. "I'll ask Wulf to send a car to the airport to expedite our trip."

Chapter Fifty-Seven

WHAT KIND OF CLUB

Rox drove them all to the airport to get on—and she still had a hard time wrapping her head around *this*—Arthur's private plane.

When they were walking out of the restaurant, Rox managed to get Cash alone outside the door for a moment while Arthur and Maxence bickered like only old school friends can: every comment was a barb pointed at painful childhood traumas.

She stood outside the door and checked, but the other two guys were far back. Cash wove his arm around her waist.

"So," Rox put a lilt in her voice to make her question sound nonchalant even though she totally wasn't, "Do you know what kind of club those guys were talking about?"

Cash said, "Yes."

"So, I—*seriously?*"

"Yes."

"I don't think I want to know how you know."

"Those kinds of clubs are common in Europe. Less so here, but more common than you would think."

"I am afraid to ask how common they are." She looked far off into the early night, where a line of street lamps dotted a trail down the dark street.

Cash said, "There are five that I know of in Los Angeles."

"No."

"Absolutely."

"That *you* know of?" Rox really should shut up.

"Yes. Are you sure that you want to go to this one?"

"I'm just making sure that you boys don't get into real trouble."

"Oh, they will."

"I'm not going to partake."

"Then why are you going?" He encroached on her, trailing his knuckles down her cheek and the side of her neck. His voice was lower, more baritone, when he whispered, "Do you want to know what goes on there?"

"Oh, heavens. I'm sure that I wouldn't know what to do. I'm sure that I would make a fool of myself."

"How many boyfriends have you had, Rox?"

"I don't know. Six, maybe? Seven?"

"And how many of those were *real* boyfriends? That's how Americans ask about sexual partners, yes?"

"Um, yes. That's how we say it without saying

it." She watched her toes, and her restless feet couldn't seem to stay still on the sidewalk.

"So how many *real* boyfriends have you had, Rox?"

"Including you?"

"Yes."

"Oh. Well. *Um.* Three."

"Including me?"

"Yes. Oh, now you think badly of me."

"No, I don't. Did either of the other ones want to do anything unusual?"

"No. Heavens. I *never."* She desperately wished that she had never started this conversation.

"Do you want me to show you what goes on at those kinds of clubs?" he asked again. "Perhaps in a private room?"

Rox swallowed. Her whole body felt like she had the wiggles. "Yes."

Chapter Fifty-Eight

THE DOM OF THE DEVILHOUSE

HARD WORK

CASIMIR

BLAIR BABYLON

At the airport, six men met them inside the terminal, all wearing nearly identical black suits and sunglasses, even inside and at night. They nodded to Maxence, who greeted them with a smile and shook their hands, and then they kept to themselves the rest of the night.

Rox kept an eye on them, but they sipped soda water and played cards as if they didn't all smell subtly like gunpowder.

Southern girls pick up on those things. She edged closer to Cash.

The small jet seated twelve people in large, lounger-style seats. The creamy leather was spotless and embroidered on each seat with an ornate *S*.

Considering Arthur, Rox assumed that the *S* stood for Slytherin.

Two of Maxence's security men took the first two seats, but the rest went to the rear of the plane, flanking him. They left Maxence alone so he could talk with Arthur, Cash, and Rox in the center of the plane for the rest of the flight.

Rox wondered at it, chewing over why Maxence rated a security team while Arthur and Cash did not, and that odd conversation among the men that first day popped up in her head again.

Maxence had "dynastic problems."

Cash had escaped his.

Arthur seemed less concerned.

Rox worried at the concept of "dynastic problems" like a ferret that had found an odd smell to obsess over while the guys talked sports. College football season was in full swing, but they seemed more concerned with the rugby international World Cup. Arthur was being very modest in the discussion, and Maxence, flippant. Rox figured that England was a powerhouse, the Netherlands were in the middle, and Monaco had a weak team.

They flew for a little over an hour, a silver wasp darting through the night sky, and landed in the middle of a splash of city lights.

Inside a small, private terminal with no security station that Rox could see, a man was waiting for them, dressed in a night-black suit only a few shades darker than his skin. Unusual bulges near his armpits hindered his arms.

He watched them and noted each of them, especially the six men who had surrounded Maxence as they had entered the terminal. Maxence's security men focused on the man and tightened into a defensive position.

The man in the black suit approached them, his back ramrod straight as if he were ex-military. "Gentlemen, I am Jeffrey Jackson. I was sent to escort you this evening."

One of Maxence's men moved forward. He was the smallest of the six of them and more wiry than stacked. "Hugo Faure. We spoke on the phone." His accent sounded like a Frenchy kind of Italian.

"Ah," Mr. Jackson said, shaking Faure's hand and looking straight at him. "Very pleased to meet you, sir."

Hugo Faure nodded. "And you as well, sir."

It was kind of weird that they were sir-sirring each other, and Rox got the impression that something military was passing between them.

Cash stepped forward with his hand out. "I'm Casimir van Amsberg. This is Rox, Arthur, and Maxence." He nodded to each as he introduced them.

Mr. Jackson shook Cash's hand and nodded at each. "This way."

Jackson led them to three SUVs that were idling in the parking lot. Maxence waved as his black-suited men cut him out of the herd and bustled him to one of the waiting cars.

The drive through the city was quick, and Cash rested his arm on the back of the seat behind her the whole way. She leaned into him, still wondering what she had gotten herself into.

They arrived at a big, white building that looked

like a Southern plantation mansion straight out of *Gone with the Wind.*

Rox whispered to Cash, "I thought this was a—"

He squeezed her hand, and Rox shut up, even though she was pretty sure that Mr. Jackson knew what the place was, too.

The SUVs let them off at the front door, where upward-facing floodlights lit the columns, windows, and ornate trim.

Mr. Jackson emerged from the driver's seat and tossed the keys to another black-suited man as he walked around the front of the vehicle, who then drove off in the SUV and left them at the door.

Rox rubbed her arms in the chilly night air and turned back to the front door.

Another man was standing in the open doorway, lit from the interior lights behind him and the floodlights outside. He was very tall, probably six-four again, just like Cash and his school buddies. The new guy wore a dark blue suit, just like they all had a penchant for dark suits, but he was pale blond. His hair looked pale gold in the sharp downward-shining lights, and when he looked up at her, his eyes were startling, so dark blue that their blueness verged on violet when he glanced away from her to look at Arthur on the other side of Cash.

There was no kindness in the blond man's eyes when he had looked at her, just calculation. Rox edged closer to Cash, half-hiding behind him.

Cash walked more quickly down the white hallway, his footsteps muffled by the thick blue carpet under Rox's feet, and he held out his hand as he approached. "Hello!"

No name, Rox noted. Usually, Cash led with people's names because he remembered them all.

The blond man took a few steps toward them, hand extended. Even his smile was so cold that Rox's skin prickled in goosebumps. Not a whit of warmth reached his eyes.

"Casimir," he said and shook Cash's hand. He touched his own cheek, the mirror of the side of his face where Cash still had a white bandage taped over his cheek. "Everything all right?"

"Oh, yeah," Cash said. "No problem."

He nodded and turned to the other two guys. "Arthur, Maxence. Pleasure to see you after so long."

"Yes, it's been far too long," Arthur said, a grin widening his mouth. "Weeks, at least."

"Indeed. I haven't seen you for years, Maxence. Not anywhere."

That seemed loaded.

Rox looked up from her short-girl stature, watching the men who towered over her. They must feed them growth hormones at that school they all went to. From the heady amount of testosterone swirling among them that Rox swore she could smell, it was probably Brahma bull growth hormone.

Cash turned to her and bent, his hand extended toward the blond man. "Rox, this is The Dom of The Devilhouse. You can call him Sir or Dom."

Was Cash serious? She had heard about books that dealt with stuff like that but hadn't read them.

Okay, she hadn't read very many of them.

Cash stood and spoke to The Dom. "This is Roxanne Neil. She's with me."

That last part sounded a little sharp, kind of like the time that Cash had told opposing counsel that he and Rox would not be attending the stripper party.

The Dom bent slightly to shake her hand. For the minute that he looked into her eyes, his dark blue eyes seemed to take in all of her.

She croaked, "Pleased to meet you."

"And a pleasure to meet you," The Dom said, still looking straight into her eyes. When she looked into his dark blue eyes, the color brightened to a cobalt shade of blue, almost glowing.

Rox withdrew her hand from his and stepped closer to Cash again, even though she couldn't seem to look away from The Dom's stare.

The Dom straightened and turned back to Arthur, breaking their eye contact. "Come with me, gentlemen," he shot a small, cold smile at her, "and lady. I thought a drink in my office first?"

"Yes, Sir," Arthur said.

Rox swore that she could hear the capital letter.

She followed the guys through the white-painted hallways and steeled herself for whatever kind of kinky and weird accoutrement that a sex club owner would fill his office with. She sucked in a fortifying breath as she walked through the door, but his office had a conversation grouping of blue couches around a coffee table at the back and a glass-topped desk at the other end. A long, wide window looked out into the night at, Rox assumed, the park area that the driveway had meandered through before cars had dropped them off at the front doors.

Anti-climactic.

She followed Cash to one of the couches and sat beside him, his unbandaged cheek toward her.

He tucked her against his side, curling his strong arm around her.

Any other time, she might have bristled at the possessive move, but The Dom turned back to them and pinned her to the couch with one stare.

She huddled closer to Cash, nearly winding herself around his leg and trim waist.

The Dom sat on the couch opposite them. "Drinks will be here shortly. Casimir, I assume that you'll want a private room."

Cash nodded and tightened his arm around Rox.

The Dom continued, "Arthur and Maxence, you have a few minutes before your appointments."

Arthur grinned.

Maxence twitched in his chair. "I don't need an appointment tonight."

The Dom raised one blond eyebrow at him. "She'll be disappointed that you cancelled."

Arthur laughed out loud and leaned back in his chair.

The office door opened, and a short woman

came in. Her natural hair fuzzed around her head, and she wore the tightest, shortest business skirt suit that Rox had ever seen on a human rather than a fashion doll. She carried a wide tray crowded with glasses and decanters filled with amber or clear liquid.

The Dom glanced up at her. "Thank you, Glenda."

When she smiled, her dark plum lips opened to reveal white teeth. She set the tray on the coffee table and adjusted her skirt before she turned to leave.

As soon as the door closed behind her, Maxence said, "I can't."

"That's understandable," The Dom said. His deep voice was as light as Rox had heard it so far, a non-judgmental tone. He leaned forward and poured different liquors into each of the tumblers and one glass of white wine.

Cash took a tumbler for himself and handed her the wine glass. Rox sipped, tasting the sweet note and then caramel finish of a very good wine. *Delicious.* She gulped half the glass.

"I *shouldn't,*" Maxence said to The Dom again.

"That's up to you," The Dom said.

"It's using a person as a plaything, a pawn. I *can't.*"

"I don't think of Mairearad as a pawn or a plaything, and I assure you, you shouldn't call her that."

Maxence was sitting on the edge of his chair,

holding both his hands open. "But it is. This is all superficial. It's manipulative. It's *evil.*"

"Why don't you ask Mairearad about what she thinks? I wouldn't want to speak for her."

Maxence flinched backward.

Rox was impressed. This Dom guy would have been a good litigator.

"Indeed," The Dom said, "you've already booked her for this time slot. It would be impolite to cancel. I suggest you have a drink with her and ask what she thinks."

"She'll say whatever she thinks I want to hear," Maxence grumbled.

The Dom's blond eyebrows rose a fraction of an inch. "I doubt that." A knock rattled the door. "Ah, here she is."

Maxence flopped back in his chair. His wary glance at the door looked grim.

Rox tried to formulate a plan to get him out of this situation. Surely she could say something that he could pick up on so that he could escape.

A woman strutted into the office, her ebony ponytail twitching as she walked. Her black business pantsuit shone in the recessed lighting, and it took Rox just a second to realize that it was made of leather. Discreet silver studs sparkled at the pockets.

The woman smiled at the four men, her dark red lips contrasting her pale skin. She looked vampiric. "Gentlemen," she said in a low, sultry voice.

Oh. My. God.

The Dom said, "Maxence, this is Mairearad."

When Rox glanced back, Maxence's dark eyes were wide, and his hands were knotted into fists on the arms of the chair. He didn't look angry. His eyes looked hungrily at the woman, and he uncurled his fingers to clutch the upholstery, looking like he was holding on by his fingernails to keep himself from flinging himself across the room at her.

Mairearad's smile at Maxence looked like she knew all his secrets just by looking at him. "Hello, Maxence."

Maxence rose from his chair as if he were hypnotized. "I should like to ask you some questions. That's all."

"Of course," she said and walked to the door. "Follow me."

Maxence followed her. "I just want to ask you some questions," he repeated.

She turned back, and her voice was more gentle. "Let's talk in my office."

Maxence's shoulders drooped in relief. "Yes, your office."

He followed her out and shut the door behind himself.

Arthur laughed. "How long do you think they will actually talk?"

The Dom checked his phone. "Ah, here comes your consultant, Arthur."

The office door opened again, and another woman came in. This girl was wearing jeans and a silk blouse, buttoned all the way up to her neck. Her blond hair was tied back in a messy knot on the back of her head, and her loose-limbed gait looked like she was gamboling through her own house.

Rox blinked. The two women could not have been more dissimilar.

The woman smiled a brilliant smile that felt like sunshine on a summer's day and looked right at Arthur. "Ready?"

"Oh, yes," Arthur said, pushing himself up from the chair. "Hello, Chloe. I was hoping you would be free."

She grinned and held out her hand to him, not like for a handshake but to hold her hand. He reached for her hand, and she led him away, asking, "What movie did you pick?"

"Another rom-com," Arthur said, just before the door closed behind him. *"Love and Whiskey."*

"That sounds lovely! I've got popcorn ready to pop, too."

"Splendid."

Rox glanced up at Cash. "All right, I think I know what Maxence just got himself in for, but was Arthur speaking in code or something?"

"I don't think so," Cash said. "He was looking at movie reviews in the car."

"I just can't even—never mind. I don't want to know." Her voice still sounded shaky.

The Dom was watching her again. He thumbed something on his phone. "Casimir, you have your pick of rooms tonight, as it's a Monday. Before you take Rox back, why don't you peruse them and decide which one is appropriate."

The office door opened, and Glenda stood there again, smiling at them. Rox didn't know how she could breathe in that skin-tight suit, but at least it looked good on her. She didn't have any pudge.

The Dom said, "Glenda can show you the options."

Cash told her, "That's a good idea. I'll be back in one minute."

Rox pointedly did not glance at The Dom over there on the other couch. "You think that's a good idea?"

"There are some very different options," he said. "I think I should look."

"Okay."

"I'll be right back." Cash followed the small woman who pranced ahead of him on stiletto heels, and the door clicked shut behind him, leaving her alone with the very imposing figure of The Dom.

Rox glanced back at him, her eyes suddenly too wide on her face.

"I wanted to talk to you alone," he said, his blue eyes right on her and staring again. They seemed bright blue again, so intense.

"Oh?" she asked, trying to steady her voice.

He said, "You don't have to do anything you don't want to do."

"I know that," she said, shrinking back into the seat. If he came at her, she was a Southern girl and she could fight off any man, given half a chance. Her breath sped up, and frightened heat flashed across her face.

The Dom leaned forward and braced his forearms on his knees, clasping his hands. "I mean tonight, here, with Casimir. You have been shaking ever since you walked into the building. When you picked up your glass, the wine vibrated, and then you drank it as if you were trying to fortify yourself. You look pale and terrified. If Casimir is going too far, too fast, I can get you out of this. He will never know we spoke, and he won't be upset at you. I will find some excuse. This happens all the time. It is neither a bother nor unusual. Do you want me to do this?"

Rox's stomach uncoiled. "No, I'm okay."

"Are you sure?" he asked, still looking right at her.

"I'm sure. I'm here because I want to be."

"If you change your mind at any time, just say 'Not my cup of tea,' and we will have someone to you very quickly. Can you remember that?"

"Right," Rox said, breathing more easily. "Not my cup of tea."

"That's right."

"Do you listen in?" she asked, horrified at what that might mean.

"We have security arrangements for everyone's safety," The Dom said, settling back in his seat.

"I suppose you have to for liability reasons." She sipped her wine again.

His smile was a little less icy this time. "We are very careful, but we must be cognizant of liability issues."

"That must be interesting," she said, setting her wine glass back on the table and clasping her hands, the classic listening posture. "You must have interesting contract issues, too."

"Why, yes." He picked up his glass. "We'll need you to sign a release, of course."

"Oh, of course. I understand."

"Casimir was instrumental in writing it," he said. "There were problems early on with opening this place, and Casimir helped enormously on the legal end."

"He's a fantastic lawyer."

"He is, indeed. I always have him look over my contracts, and I'd love to have him do more of my negotiations. He can talk anyone into anything, even if the idea is anathema to them." He glanced at his phone screen. "And here he is."

Cash opened the door, and Rox saw Glenda walking away down the hall. "I've secured a room for us."

"Okay." The trembling started in Rox's chest again.

"You can drop by my office afterward, if you like," The Dom told her, "for a drink or a cup of tea."

Chapter Fifty-Nine

WULF WATCHES

The Dom, for he even thought of himself by that name when he was in The Devilhouse, opened the door to the security room. "Mr. Jackson?"

"Yes, Sir?" Jeffrey Jackson answered.

His chief of security was half-reclining in a large office chair set before a bank of monitors. Each of the screens showed a wide-angle shot of a room on the premises. As it was Monday night, most showed a grainy image of unoccupied furniture or equipment.

The Dom watched the rooms that Arthur and Maxence were in for a moment. "They are all right?"

"All the usual," Jeffrey said, pointing one stout finger toward the screen. "They just walked in."

Casimir and Roxanne had just walked into Play Room Two, a fairly typical dungeon-style room.

The Dom watched the woman wrap her arms

around herself. "I have concerns about that one." He pointed to a screen where Roxanne stood, her arms hugged around herself. "I've given her a signal, 'not my cup of tea.' Someone should be stationed outside that door, and if you hear that, they go in immediately."

He picked up his radio. "You think she was coerced?"

"I think Casimir could talk anyone into just about anything. I want her protected."

"I've got a skeleton crew on tonight."

The Dom paused. "We'll use one of my private security for the evening. I'll have Dieter pick up a radio."

Chapter Sixty
THE DEVILHOUSE

Rox followed Cash through the white hallways, trying not to look like she was gawking at every stupid thing in the sex club.

The hallway and doors looked so ordinary, so office-like, other than that the high ceiling hung much farther above her head than in an ordinary office building. The lighting fixtures were even higher up the walls than normal.

Oh, high ceilings.

When Arthur and Maxence had been joking about "high ceilings," they had meant that Cash knew a lot about *sex clubs.* They must all be built with tall ceilings or something.

She snickered.

Cash turned. "What?"

"Nothin'," but she grinned at him.

He raised one eyebrow at her but kept walking.

Cash stopped at a door, opened it, and stood to the side, holding it for her.

She walked in and stepped aside, keeping close to the wall. Hot air wafted around her.

Odd, that the room was so warm. Her business suit seemed like too many layers of thick cloth for the small room. Anybody wearing normal clothes in here would sweat through their clothes in no time.

Oh.

She got it.

They had evidently come in the back door of the dungeon because the first thing that Rox saw when her eyes adjusted to the gloom was an enormous, carved door on the opposite side of the room like a doorway to Hell.

Cash closed the door behind them. When she turned around, the door was camouflaged, painted into the stone-bricked wall. Sconces on the walls glowed with orange bulbs as if they were pitch torches.

And there were apparatuses stationed around the room, odd skeletal structures like weird gym equipment that were empty of weights.

Her arms warmed, and she realized that Cash was standing right behind her, touching her.

She said, "I don't know how anything in here is supposed to work."

Cash ran his hands up her neck. "I do."

His voice was about half an octave lower than usual, and it had a calmness, an unswaying determination that he didn't usually have.

She cleared her throat. "Somehow, that isn't reassuring."

"It should be." He stroked the back of her neck with his fingers. "Dilettantes get hurt in places like this. You're safe with me."

"Am I?"

"You're always safe with me."

"I'm a little scared," she admitted.

He wrapped his arms around her from behind. "We can leave. We'll go have a drink with The Dom and wait for Arthur and Maxence."

"Give me a minute."

The black iron and silver contraptions jutted into the air, shining and yet dark at the same time. Ropes and whips and spiked metal torture things hung in glass cases.

Rox clasped her hands in front of her. "Do you want to hurt me?"

"No."

"Those things over there look like they're for hurting people."

"That's not the point," he said. "Unless you are both into that sort of thing, you shouldn't hurt the other person just to hurt them."

"And you're into that sort of thing, hurting people."

"No. I don't like sadism or masochism. Everything done here should heighten the other person's reaction so that when the pleasure comes—and it should—it is that much sweeter and more intense."

Cruel whips and ties and chains and metal bars crowded the room. "Just looking at all this is making me nuts."

Cash gently turned her around so that she faced the wall. "Then don't look."

"It doesn't mean that all that stuff just disappeared. Just because I'm not looking at it doesn't mean that it's not there. Just because you refuse to acknowledge something doesn't mean that it isn't going to happen."

He pressed her shoulders, moving her closer to the wall, and then blocked her view of the room with his broad shoulders. "But most of it doesn't concern you. On your first day at Arbeitman, Silverman, and Amsberg, I didn't hand you a stack of contracts and tell you to have them annotated and back to me by the next morning."

She shook her head. "We sat down together, across from each other at a table, with several contracts and talked about important paragraphs and how you wanted me to handle something like that."

"And how did you feel about that, afterward?"

"Confident," she said, closing her eyes at the memory. He had gazed at her with those glamorous green eyes of his all day and spoken softly, smiling when she picked up on something. "Like I knew what to do and how to do it."

"Safe," he whispered.

"Yes." Her voice was as breathy as if she was hypnotized.

"I always keep you safe."

Physically, yes.

Professionally, absolutely.

She nodded, holding all the exceptions inside.

His breath brushed the back of her neck, and the cinnamon and musk of his cologne swirled around her. "In the rest of your life, you take care of everyone, and you are responsible for everything."

"Yeah. I'm an adult. That's what adults do."

"For a few hours, give it to me."

"What?" That scared the hell out of her.

"Give it all to me. Don't worry. Don't think. Don't plan. Don't manage. Lay down all your responsibilities and your fears. For a few hours, just *feel.*"

He lifted her arms and pressed her hands against the wall above her head, palms against the cool stone.

"That sounds so old-fashioned, so—" Dang it, she couldn't quite think of the right word, not with his heavy body warming her back and pressing her against the wall. "Let the man do whatever he wants to you. Lie still and think of England."

He chuckled low in his throat. "You won't be able to lie still, I assure you."

"It sounds like you'll be doing all the work. Planning all the things."

"I'll do that."

"Like you'll have all the control."

"Yes. That's exactly it." His warm lips pressed the place where her shoulder met her neck. *"Breathe."* He ran his hands up her arms and pressed her hands flat against the wall. "Trust me."

A trembling started deep in her chest. "Trust you?"

"Close your eyes. Just breathe."

"How do I know that you won't just tie me up and leave me here, helpless?"

"You'll have to trust me."

Rox sucked her lower lip into her mouth and bit down.

"Think of this: in three years, have I ever betrayed you? Have I ever not been there for you when you needed me?"

"You screwed a buttload of other women." Her tone was a little drier than she had meant it to be.

"You were married, or you said that you were. You do not get to be angry about that."

"Yeah, well, *that.*" This was why she was not a litigator's paralegal. Her arguments were stupid when she was all het up.

He said, "I ran myself to the ground, trying to keep my hands off of you, to keep myself from seducing you into breaking your vows."

He sure thought a lot of himself that he just assumed that she would fall on her back and break her fictional wedding vows if he had crooked his little finger at her.

And yet, the moment he had put his arms around her on the deck, she had fallen for all his games.

She said, "Yeah, screwing all those women must have been rough on you, poor baby."

His deep voice vibrated near her skin. "But I've

always been there whenever you needed me, no matter what happened. Together, we assaulted a man in Athens when he tried to hurt you."

A huge man had grabbed her, thrown her up against a wall, and groped her boobs. She had kneed him in the nutsack, but the guy hadn't gone down. If anything, it had made him angrier, and the liquor on his breath had made her dizzy. Cash had spun him around and cold-cocked him in the jaw, slamming the guy to the ground.

She said, "Um, yeah."

"And I carried you across that river in Brazil."

"I couldn't believe those other lawyers insisted on that hike. The current was too strong. I couldn't keep my feet. I didn't want to see Sting's rain forest quite *that* closely."

"I have always been there when you needed me. I've always protected you and kept you safe. I will tonight, too."

She couldn't seem to breathe all the way down into her lungs. "But what if you can't? What if something happens? What if it turns out that I'm allergic to nylon or whatever those ropes are made out of?"

Twisted skeins of ropes hung in a glass-front case, sorted by color and thickness. They reminded Rox of her great-aunt's knitting yarn stash and yet were so different and freaky.

He whispered, "You're arguing to argue. First, you tried to argue the law, saying that the underlying theory was retrogressive—"

Yeah, *retrogressive.* That was the word she had been looking for, dang it. Trust the European guy who had learned high-falutin' English to take the vocab-heavy Law School Admissions Test to know the twenty-dollar word.

"—but I refuted your logic. Then, you argued the facts of the case, saying that you couldn't trust me. When I rebutted that with concrete examples, you began to just argue, throwing out a squirrel case about the allergenic qualities of the ropes."

He chuckled against her neck, and then his teeth nipped her skin. A shiver passed through Rox, and she let her head fall back against his strong shoulder.

His hands curled over hers, high above her head.

"Here is your choice: you said that you wanted me to teach you what goes on in these clubs. You'll have to give up all responsibility and control to me. You'll have to trust me to know you, to do it right, and to stop if that's what needs to happen."

It seemed like too much to ask, and yet, the thought of laying down her burdens for just a few hours was unreasonably attractive. "Okay."

His voice near her neck was almost a whisper, "You have to say, 'I submit.'"

She sucked in a breath to argue about those words, but he was right. She was arguing just to argue.

Rox swallowed hard to get rid of the worried lump in her throat and choked out, "I submit."

He dragged his hands down her skin and

wrapped her in his arms. "Thank you. It's a gift, for you to give up control to me."

She nodded, feeling smaller and more helpless in his burly arms than she ever had before. His biceps, pressing on her upper arms, seemed larger, more powerful, like he could grab her weaker body and break her into pieces if he felt like it.

He said, "You need to pick a safe word."

"I don't know what that is. I don't know anything about this." Her voice was still a bit soprano with panic.

He said, "A word to signal true distress, a failsafe that you will say if you are overwhelmed, if you want me to stop everything and untie you."

"Oh, okay. That seems fair." Her voice felt a little stronger.

"You need to pick one."

"Um, can't you pick one?"

"No. You have to do this."

"Okay. *Um. Caveat?"*

"Latin for a warning. That is an excellent one. Would you like one that means that you are in some discomfort, that means not to stop, but to be careful or to modify what I am doing?"

"Yeah. Yeah, that's a good idea."

"And it would be?" She could hear the smile in his voice.

"Sub modo," she said.

"*Sub modo,* to modify a contract with agreement of all parties. Good. Now turn around." He stepped back enough for her to pivot.

Rox turned around, but he was still standing so close to her. The cold, stone wall was right behind her, and she leaned back against it. Chill passed through her clothes and trailed along her spine and butt like a ghost.

"Good." He touched her chin, lifting her face with his fingers.

He positioned her head where he wanted it, tilting her face a little to the right.

This kind of control, this micromanaging, felt alien. She was used to managing people. She was used to working *with* him.

This vulnerability felt like an invasion into her mind.

He kissed her, gently, almost lovingly.

She really shouldn't think things like *lovingly.* Like Wren had said, Cash was all about fun and games. This control thing, this dominance-submission thing, must be just another game to him.

His lips caressed hers, and she melted against him.

He nudged her backward with his mouth, bracing himself with his hand on the wall behind her, and pressed his body against hers. Luckily, she was still wearing her high heels, so he didn't have to bend down ridiculously far.

Her hands crept up, finding first the strong cords of his abdominals around his waist, then the smooth rounds of his pecs and shoulders.

He was even kissing her differently tonight.

Usually, or at least before, when he had kissed her, his mouth had devoured her, an expression of passion and lust. It had only been a few weeks since the first time he had kissed her in his bedroom, when she had tried to rip that bandage off of his cheek.

Tonight, his lips caressed hers, lightly sucked at her lower lip, and his tongue stroked hers, but it all seemed deliberate, calculated. The bandage on his cheek didn't brush her face at all.

He traced her arms to her wrists and lifted her hands away from his neck, placing them at her sides and pressing her hands against her thighs.

"I want—" she began, her lips still against his.

"Let me," he growled.

He held her hands against her own soft thighs and kissed her, his mouth straying to her jaw and shoulder but returning to her lips.

She wanted her arms around him. She wanted to touch him and finally lick those tattoos that flamed along his left side from his muscled shoulder to his corded thigh.

His broad chest pushed against her, pressing her back against the wall. Cold stole through her blouse, freezing her back and butt.

He stepped back and pulled her with him, leading her with his hands and his lips.

She followed him, walking blindly.

In the center of the room, Cash settled his hand on her shoulder, stopping her. "I'm going to undress you now."

She nodded, even though she had a feeling that she didn't need to.

He took his own shirts off first, unbuttoning the neck of his dress shirt and pulling it and his undershirt over his head, baring the dark flames of the tattoo on the left side of his body and the three shields arranged on his right forearm. His body undulated with muscle as he stripped, all those thick ropes of muscle moving under his skin like he was dancing. He pressed the bandage back onto his cheek after the shirts had snagged it.

Rox tried to look like she wasn't staring, but she totally was. As he peeled his sleeves down his arms, baring his thick forearms with a thin veil of brown hair on them, she couldn't look away. Dark, tattooed fire gripped his skin all down his left arm and covered the inverted triangle of his lats to the waistband of his suit slacks.

He tossed his shirts on the floor and turned back to her. His hands rose to her suit jacket.

She had planned a solid meeting at the office and a nice, quiet supper with Maxence and Arthur. How had she ended up on a private jet and then in a sex club in another state?

Insanity.

Cash smoothed his hands over her shoulders, pushing her jacket back and down her arms. He caught it before it fell off of her hands and laid it over a crossbar on a thing that looked like a gym's pull-up tower.

He walked around her like he was inspecting her,

but his fingers kept darting out to touch her, to caress her skin on her bare arms or the back of her neck.

When he came around to stand in front of her again, he reached for the hem of her shirt, sliding his fingers underneath, touching her waist, then lifting it over her head.

His eyes dipped, noticing her pale blue silk bra. "I do like this one."

"You've already seen it once today. You'd think you'd be sick of it by now."

He touched his fingers to her lips. "No talking except to say one of your safe words."

"I beg your—"

"No talking." An evil twinkle lit in his green eyes. "Or I'll turn you over my knee and spank you."

Her mouth dropped open. "You *wouldn't.*"

His smile widened a little. "Are you trying to make me spank you?"

Rox felt her breath stop in her chest, and she shook her head no.

"Then let's not play that game." He walked around behind her and unbuttoned her skirt's closure at her waist. His warm fingers dipped inside her waistband, and her skirt loosened as he unzipped it. The fabric dropped to the floor, baring her matching blue silk underwear.

She felt his fingers stroke her hips, lightly rubbing the lace that stretched over her skin.

"Step out of the skirt."

She did, still wearing her high heels and nothing

else except wispy underwear.

Behind her, Cash sucked in a breath.

Warmth covered her back, and he whispered near her ear. "Thank you for allowing me to do this."

Something like happiness suffused through her. She nodded.

Cash slid his hands from her shoulders to her hips and rocked her back against himself, running his hands over her.

He whispered, "I love how soft your skin is."

Rox leaned against him, relaxing into his massage.

Cash's firm palms stroked her, sliding over her body from her shoulders and down her arms, then he circled her waist. He rubbed down her hips, almost dancing with her, but one hand drifted upward and across her chest to cup her breast through her thin bra. Even with his huge hands, she overflowed his fingers.

His other hand stole lower, lightly stroking her folds over her panties.

Rox sighed and let her head fall back against his shoulder.

"That's good, *lieveke.* Relax. Let me hold you."

He pulsed his fingers around her breast, almost pulling at her but he was too gentle for it to hurt at all.

With each grasp, his hand slid farther down her breast until he drew his fingers over her nipple, and she stretched, pushing against his hand.

"Don't move," he whispered. "Just stand still. Feel me."

Rox tried to comply. She really did. His hands loved her skin, holding handfuls of her body like he was gathering every bit of her to himself. His fingertips brushed her clit, and even over the silk of her panties, a shiver tightened inside her.

She moaned.

His whispered shush near her neck floated along her shoulder.

He moved one hand behind her to unhook her bra. The straps slipped over her arms. He caught the scrap of silk and tossed it near the growing pile of clothes on the tile floor. Both his hands caressed her hips, sliding under the lace of her underwear, and he worked them down her thighs until they fell.

"Step out."

She lifted her feet, her high heels clicking on the rough tile. Cash flicked the panties toward the pile of clothes.

His hands roamed her naked skin now, caressing and almost pinching her nipples and clit, always on the verge of hurting her but never quite sliding over from intense sensation to pain. She swayed on her high-heeled pumps, the only things that she was wearing.

A pinch to both her nipples shot a burst of pleasure through her, and her knees buckled. Though she caught herself, his arms swooped around her, and he lifted her to his bare chest.

She started to grab his neck, but Cash shook his

head. Rox crossed her fists over her bare breasts, and he took all of her weight with his arms. He carried her as easily as if she were a kitten, looking into her eyes the whole time. The dim, golden light turned his eyes impossibly dark green.

Passion hummed in her blood, but being carried so easily made her feel so small, so *helpless.* She laid her head on his shoulder, huddling closer to him.

He lowered her, and her naked butt touched something padded. She wasn't hanging on to his neck so she didn't need to let go, but she adjusted herself as his arms withdrew.

Cash stroked her cheek, still looking into her eyes. "Lie back."

She reached and touched the bench beside her thighs. Her fingers found rails along the side of the bench, and she held on as she leaned back. Cash had a small smile on his face, and he watched her, seeming to approve.

The bench-thing rose behind her lower back as she let herself lean back, but it bent down behind her as she lay back farther.

Rox glanced behind herself, unsure.

The bench curved back like a bridge, so that she would be bowed backward across it. Between her legs, the seat of the bench had been cut away so that someone could stand there, or whatever. At least the manufacturer had thought that through.

When she turned back, Cash's eyes were inches from hers. He had leaned over and was bracing himself on the rails to stare at her. The white bandage on his left cheek glowed in the flickering lights. "Lie back."

"Okay." Her voice shook a little, but she inched backward, lengthening her neck as she stretched across the bench. The leather upholstery cooled her naked back. Her legs hung over the end, but she braced her high heels on tile floor. Her head fell back. Blood rushed behind her eyes, and she looked over her boobs at him.

Cash was still leaning over her, watching her lie back. His gaze traveled downward toward her boobs and waist, and a glimmer stole into his green eyes. As he looked down her body, he sucked one side of his lower lip into his mouth and bit it.

Wow.

When he looked up at her, his grin reached all the way to his eyes, and he leaned down and kissed her stomach without looking away.

Without thinking, she reached out and cradled his cheek in her hand.

He turned his head and kissed the heel of her hand, but then he held her wrist and pushed up, still gripping her wrist. "I said, don't touch me."

He pushed himself off her and walked around where she lay, holding her arm in the air, and pressed her hand to the rail above her head.

"Hold on," he said, looking into her eyes again. "Don't let go. Stay just like that."

She nodded and held onto the cold rail.

Cash walked over to one of the cabinets, the one that was filled with twisted skeins of rope.

Rox watched him walk away. Light from the sconces shone on his bare shoulders and the bulges of his back, and his tight butt flexed under his suit slacks as he strode over to the case. She had watched that ass for years, wanting to grab it. Now that she had had her hands all over it, she knew that it was indeed as rock hard as it looked under that light wool suit fabric that always clung to the hollows of his ass cheeks.

At the rope cabinet, his fingers walked among the smaller knots on the top row. The bright strands twitched as he touched them. He picked two scarlet ropes, lifting them from their hooks, and walked back to her with them clenched in his fist.

Cash stood above her head, and she watched him unfurl the ropes.

She pressed her lips together, keeping herself from asking what the heck he was going to do.

"Anything to say?" he asked.

Rox shook her head no. She wasn't going to invoke her safe word.

But she wanted to ask what he was planning to do with the ropes.

She didn't have to wait long.

He lashed her wrists to iron loops that jutted out from the sides of the bench just above her ears.

When he was done, he walked past her to her feet.

The ropes held firm when Rox twisted her hands, but they didn't tighten. If she let her hands go limp, she couldn't even feel the ropes.

Down by her feet, Cash picked up her ankles and bent her knees to fold her legs, and he gently spread her thighs until she felt some kind of footrest through the shoes. He tied her ankles to yet more loops that she hadn't noticed.

This felt very, *very* helpless. Rox swallowed hard and held down the snake of panic that had climbed into her throat.

Cash ran his hands up her legs and her thighs, stroking her.

Rox looked up at the ceiling, willing her hot eyes to stay dry. If she let a tear leak out, he would see it, and she didn't want him to see. She wasn't weak like that.

His hands on her legs, kneading and rubbing her flesh, that felt so very, *very* good.

"You're tense," he said.

Yeah. No kidding. She adjusted her legs as much as the ties would allow her.

He said, "For tonight, give up all your responsibility and control. Don't worry. Let it all go. I'll take care of everything, *lieveke.* I'll take care of *you.*"

She should try.

Rox's body lengthened on the bench as her arms and legs relaxed.

Cash chuckled, massaging her legs and up her sides. "That's better."

Rox twisted her hands in the ropes and found that she could reach the iron loops. She clutched them like handles.

His hands roamed her legs, massaging her calves

and the tops of her feet. With her head hanging down the other side of the bench, she couldn't see him unless she curled up, pulling on her wrists bound above and behind her. When she tried, her arms weighed her down. Holding herself up was exhausting, and her abs began to tremble within seconds.

Rox lay back while his hands traveled over her skin.

His strong fingers caressed her thighs, milking the tension out of them. With each swipe of his hands, her body relaxed, until his hands began to reach higher on her legs.

As his hands swirled, each rub brought them closer to her sex.

She began to anticipate each stroke, feeling his large, strong hands press her legs, run up her flesh, and she closed her eyes.

His strong hands rose up her legs again, and this time, he brushed his fingers over her folds.

Her body was still responding to him from when he was holding her in his arms, still ripe from his touch, and a jolt blew through her.

She arched off the bench, and his chuckle floated through the air to her.

His hands firmed on her inner thighs, massaging, and his thumbs parted her folds, barely touching her, giving her only the smallest of touches when she craved much more.

As she sighed, and then moaned, he touched her more, stroked her more, *teased* her more.

One of his thumbs rubbed a tight circle over her clit, tightening her body. The other pushed inside her, rubbing her *there,* deepening every stroke.

She whimpered and tightened her fists on the handles.

Her body knotted, getting close. Her thighs trembled as she arched, feeling every stroke. His relentless rhythm drove her closer to the edge. Her breath rushed in her lungs.

So close.

His hands slowed, withdrew, and massaged her legs.

Rox opened her eyes. "Why did you—"

He was smiling over her bare knees at her. "No talking, or I will spank you."

Even though he was still smiling that intense, sly smile, his green eyes were perfectly serious.

Her abs started to shake again. Rox lay back on the bench.

Warmth touched her knee, something warm and wet.

She curled back up and tried to brace herself on her elbows, but she couldn't quite get them to the table because her wrists were tied.

He had pressed his mouth to her knee, running his lips and tongue over the inside of her thigh. His hand was braced against her other knee, his forearm turned so she could see the tattoo of the three shields: the red and white checkerboard, the one with the three crowns on a blue field, and the last one—the one that always drew her attention—white lion, aflame, on bright orange.

Didn't the Dutch national sports teams wear orange? She seemed to remember from the last Olympics, that the Dutch team had worn glowing, neon orange.

Rox fell back, breathing hard.

The warmth of his mouth traveled up the inside of her leg, blowing humid warmth over her skin and making her thigh quiver when he reached halfway.

He nipped her then, a quick clip with his teeth that stung, and then he soothed her skin with his tongue.

Rox anticipated each tortuous lick and sucking kiss as his mouth ascended her leg. He pressed his hand to her other thigh, opening her legs farther, and the warm air cooled the damp skin between her legs.

The warmth of his mouth crawled up her thigh and over the softness at the top, and he tongued the crease between her thigh and folds before he settled his mouth on her and started with a slow lick that took forever to rub over her clit.

Rox clutched the ropes on her wrists lest she fly off the bench.

He pressed his lips on her, using his tongue and lips like a long, deeply penetrating French kiss. Her body trembled, every second a torture as she edged closer to orgasm. She pushed with her heels, lifting her hips, and he slid his hands under her ass and tongued her harder, dipping inside her and laving over every sensitive nub and spot, *all* of them.

The iron loops dug into Rox's fingers as she held on, her breath trapped in her chest. Her body spun, spiraled more tightly as the pleasure wound around her and strangled her. She gasped for air, but her lungs were straining, *almost there.*

Cold.

Nothing and cold.

Nothing.

She screamed through clenched teeth.

His mouth had left her clit, and Cash crawled up her body. He had taken his pants off at some point. A small part of her mind was impressed by his multi-tasking, but she was too dazed from the sudden lack of his mouth on her clit to think. *"Wha—"*

His cock lay on her stomach, heavy and so long, while she panted. Her body thrummed with near-release.

"Please," she whispered.

He growled, "I want to make you come with my mouth, but I am greedy. I want to feel you clench around my cock. I want you to pant my name into my mouth. I want to feel your body in my arms as you twist, helpless."

Helpless.

"Please," she whispered, nearly exhausted. A drop of sweat near her hairline ran past her ear and dropped off her jaw, and more sweat like raindrops gathered on her chest and stomach.

He stepped back—yes, he had to actually *step back*—and ran the thick head of his cock through her folds. Her skin was so tender from his hand and his mouth that she arched just with that, just with him rubbing her a little more. He bent over her, kissing her chest and breasts softly, while he pressed himself into her.

As he filled her—oh so slowly—she squeezed her eyes shut and cried out, not in pain, but because it was all so much, too much. She wanted to beg him to take her hard, to finally break her and let her come, but she was so swollen that he had to carefully, slowly, force his way into her.

Finally, just as Rox thought that she would crack open or come hard just from his insidious invasion of her body, his hips pushed against her body. He groaned and laid his forehead on her sternum, panting, *"Roxanne."*

"Cash," she whispered, her hands twisting in the ropes, *"please."*

His body moved in hers, slowly pumping into her, rubbing her clit at the top of each stroke. She was so near that every languid slide into her rubbed the inside of her all the way to the top, and she was throbbing, tightening again, so close *again.*

Still moving in her, he slid his hands up her arms, sliding on her slick skin, and held her wrists against the iron bars.

The trembling climbed inside her, her desperation for the orgasm slamming into the fear of the helplessness.

He held her down with his hands and his body and the ropes and moved inside her, and she couldn't move, couldn't touch him, couldn't breathe with wanting him to slam into her and yet the world was turning black around her.

Every movement of his body was nearly sending her over the edge but it felt like a threat, like he was almost hurting her, almost ripping her apart.

"Sub modo!" she cried out. "I can't do this. *I can't do this!"*

He flipped his hands around her wrists, ripping the ropes off her hands and switching his arms under her waist to reach the other one. He whispered, "It's okay. I've got you. I've got you. You're okay."

She curled up and grabbed his neck. "You're going to hurt me. I don't want you to hurt me."

"I'm not going to hurt you." He released her ankles with one tug on each rope and cradled her to his chest. His cock was still deep inside her. "I was never going to hurt you."

"Yes, you *are."*

He rubbed his hands down her spine and whispered, "Do you want to stop?"

Tension chained her, tight around her waist and between her legs, and she ground her body against him, so close to her release. "Please, don't stop. Just don't hurt me. Don't hurt me."

He leaned her back, one arm cinched around her waist, and stroked up into her.

A sound rumbled deep in Rox's throat, and she

lifted her hips, trying to fit herself farther over him, almost screaming her frustration.

He pushed deeper into her, and his body rubbed her clit, sending a pulse through her. She gasped and gripped him as he ground against her.

Cash growled, "I would never hurt you."

Her head spun, full of whirling passion and light. Her teeth grated in her mouth as her body clenched, *so close, so very close.* "You will," she whispered. "You're going to hurt me so much. I can't bear it."

"I won't."

She whimpered and sucked in a breath while he stroked into her. "This is all fun and games to you, but it's my heart. You're going to break my heart, and I won't be able to bear it."

He thrust up into her, shoving his body against her as her mind and body tensed down to an unbearable point of light.

One more hard thrust up into her.

And Rox crashed open.

She cried out, hanging onto him, as earthquakes shuddered through her, shaking her from her body to her mind.

She might have died except for Cash's strong arms holding her together, and she clung to him as she slowly drifted inward and opened her eyes.

"I would never hurt you," he whispered. His arms were iron bands around her.

She laid her head on his shoulder and clung to him. "I know that you say that to all the girls."

Chapter Sixty-One

ARTHUR, THE UNLIKELY VOICE OF REASON

HARD WORK

CASIMIR

2

BLAIR BABYLON

Casimir's heart was bleeding.

He knew what bleeding felt like, that cold wetness of seeping life. He had felt it too many times, and his heart ached with every thump in his chest.

Afterward, Rox had been limp in his arms, just like he had envisioned but for all the wrong reasons. Tears had streaked her face, and he had been sliced to his core.

He had carried her to the little bathroom off of the main playroom and washed her in the shower. After he had dressed her, he had brushed her hair to make her presentable.

Even so, Rox had felt like a broken doll in his hands.

He never should have brought her to The Devilhouse. He hadn't realized that she was so emotionally fragile. He had known only resilient, resourceful Rox from his office, from all their escapades and escapes, and hadn't understood that woman wasn't who Rox was.

She was the woman who would go out and buy a fake wedding ring set rather than allow her heart to be broken because it would shatter her.

He held her close in the car on the way to the airport, stroking her hair and murmuring nonsense, while Arthur prattled on about the romantic comedy movie he had watched, repeating some of the funniest lines.

At the airport, Casimir led Rox into the private terminal, where the starlit night loomed outside the wall of glass that faced the tarmac. A slender jet sped down the runway outside, lights shining into the dark, and lifted its nose as if scenting the air.

Casimir settled Rox in a cloud of an upholstered chair and asked Maxence, who had been riding with his entourage behind them, to sit with her while he spoke to Arthur for a moment.

Maxence gingerly lowered himself into the chair next to hers and, with only the briefest of concerned glances up at Casimir, spoke to her about a concert that he had seen in Paris the year before.

Rox held her head in her hands, her fingers threaded into her hair, and nodded when she should.

Arthur followed Casimir away from them.

When they were far enough away, Casimir turned and said, "I need a favor."

Arthur looked back at where Maxence was

gently, kindly talking to Rox. "What the hell did you do to that poor girl?"

Casimir stuffed one hand in his pocket and stared at the ground. "I stayed within her stated hard limits, even her soft ones. I didn't realize some other things that were going on."

"Amateurs should not play these kinds of games."

"I'm not an amateur."

"I know, I know." Arthur waved his hand, indicating he had been kidding.

"I wasn't whipping her. That wouldn't have been right for her."

"Then it was?"

Casimir ground his teeth. "Edging."

"Oh, God. I'd rather be whipped with hard leather than be brought to the brink and then not allowed to go over. Trust issues?"

"Yes." Casimir could feel himself fidgeting, a despicable habit that he thought he had long since gotten over. "Could we change the flight plan to Las Vegas tonight?"

Arthur looked back to him, his gray eyes sharp as steel. *"Why?"*

"Because I need to do this."

Arthur grabbed his shoulder. "I know that it seems like a good idea right now—"

"You don't know what went on. You don't know what she *said.*"

"It doesn't matter what *she said.* You know what you have to *do.*"

"I'm out of it. I don't have to worry about it anymore, ever again."

"If something happens to them, you mustn't give up your spot in the line of succession."

Casimir flipped his hand in the air, irritated that anyone still thought that this was an issue. "Ana will be a perfect queen. She has four children. I'm not number two anymore. I'm *sixth* in line. There is no reason for me to protect my number in the line to the throne. I never even wanted it."

"Planes crash. Terrorists make bombs." Arthur grabbed his shoulder and stared right into his eyes. "Casimir, cars can blow a tire and roll down the side of a mountain."

That wasn't fair. Every abraded scar on Casimir's body sliced him at the memory of it, even the ones sanded down to invisibility and inked over. Every healed bone ached. "You realize that you're talking about my sister and my nieces and nephews, *right?*"

"It doesn't matter whom I'm talking about."

"She has *four* children, and I don't know that she's finished. She might go for a half-dozen, for all she tells anyone."

"Willem must not be your damn king," Arthur muttered.

"It wouldn't matter even if he was. The monarch is a figurehead with ceremonial and cultural duties. We have a constitution. Even Willem couldn't hurt anyone or do anything to actually damage the Netherlands."

"If anyone could damage either the Netherlands or the monarchy itself, Willem could."

"He's not that bad. He was just a little kid."

"He's a fucking psychopath, and he always has been. He's twenty-seven now and still an asshole."

Casimir raised his hands in helplessness because you can't pick your family. "He's not as bad as when he was a kid."

"He's more subtle, if that's what you mean. If he and that freak of a wife of his have kids, for the love of God, send them to Le Rosey. Don't let them grow up around him. Even boarding school would be better than that."

Cash asked again, "Can you fly us to Vegas tonight?"

"I won't. You have to go home and lobby for an Act of Consent like everybody else. Rox will be fine. They will grumble about her being an American for all of ten minutes and then pass it. It's not like she's the daughter of a Columbian drug lord."

And even then, it had taken a few weeks, some formal receptions to meet Willem's fiancée, a couple of concessions, and the assurance that her father would not attend the wedding to pass the Act of Consent through the legislature.

"You *can't,*" Arthur said, shaking Casimir's shoulder a little. "You have to do this the correct way."

Casimir let his head drop forward, remembering how much she had been afraid that he was going to hurt her, and she hadn't meant physically. "You didn't hear what she *said.*"

"It doesn't matter what she *said.* Go to Rodeo Drive and buy her the largest diamond you can find, assure her of your love, and book a plane for Amsterdam to do the necessary things. Hell, get couples' counseling if you want to talk it out. Ana would be devastated if you eloped and lost your number. She would be pissed at you for years if you denied the Netherlands a wedding."

"Ana would understand." Eventually. She did have a penchant for correct protocol, which was not a bad quality in a figurehead queen.

"But Ariane wouldn't," Arthur said. "She will throw a tantrum for days if you deny her the opportunity to be a flower girl. She's eight, Caz. She's aging out. She doesn't have many years left to be a flower girl."

Casimir wanted to make Rox happy again and to do it now. Every fiber of his being wanted to make her smile. He craved her laugh.

But he couldn't fix Rox's fears and pain with a quick wedding, anyway. He had known that deep inside, and Arthur's arguments were the least of the reasons.

The gauze on his face itched, and he scratched around it. "There is Ariane to consider."

"That little Valkyrie will kick you in the shins if you elope and she doesn't get the chance to play flower girl."

"I might be crippled for life."

"Tell us when and where. I'll abduct Maxence from whatever fool's errand he believes will assuage his soul, and we'll stand up with you in Amsterdam or The Hague. You can't marry her tonight in Vegas, you idiot. You'll ruin everything."

Chapter Sixty-Two

LIKE THE WANING MOON

Rox lay under the covers in Casimir's bed, holding herself together with her arms and determination.

The cats slept at the very bottom of the bed, clinging to the corners. Usually, they snuggled or at least slept near her and Cash.

She must have been flopping around in her sleep.

She had been so stupid. Letting Cash's sex play provoke her into blurting out her fears and pain had been so stupid. Her own idiocy staggered her.

It was just supposed to be fun and sexy, and she'd ruined it.

He was going to break it off with her now. This was probably her last night in his bed. Tomorrow, he would find her and her three cats an apartment, and they would move her few things out, and he would ghost on her.

And she would shatter inside.

And if not tomorrow, then sometime soon. Maybe next week. Perhaps the week after.

But soon.

She could feel his absence looming as if she were watching the moon wane every night, knowing that soon there would be a moonless night of darkness.

Soon.

Stupid, stupid, stupid.

Rox found her phone on the dark nightstand and checked her social media, trying to distract herself.

Her friend Brandy Washington had posted some selfies on the shelter's social media page. Brandy's dark skin and bright white smile were centered between two new kitties, a ginger tiger and a long-haired white cat that would probably be adopted as soon as the shelter opened, even though the white cat's blue eyes were narrowed at Brandy. This picture had probably been snapped seconds before the cat attacked Brandy's nose.

Beside her, the bedcovers shifted. Cash asked, "You awake?"

Rox set her phone back on the nightstand. The screen shone blue light at the bedroom's dark ceiling. "Yeah. Look, we need to talk."

"Yes. We do." The covers moved on her chest and legs as he rolled toward her.

She sat up in the bed and rested her arms on her bent knees. "I want a safe word. When you're done, when you are going to ghost on me, I need you to say the safe word to me. Maybe, 'It's time,' or 'This has been fun.'"

"That's not what a safe word is for. A safe word means to stop."

"I need to know when *you've* stopped. I won't ask you any questions. I'll just say okay, and that's it. No pressure. No third degree. But I need to know. I need to know that you're gone. I can't be trying to get ahold of you, and you passing through my fingers like a ghost. All right?"

"I don't want this to end," he said, his deep voice rolling out of the darkness. In the dim light from her phone screen, she could just see blackness filling the hollows of his eyes and one side of his face. The bandage on his left cheek was a white splotch in the night.

"Yes, you do," she said. "I understand that. I've always known that about you. I knew what I was getting into when I kissed you that first time. I knew what I was getting into the second that I threw those fake rings over the side of the deck. I won't pry. I won't interrogate you afterward. I just need a signal. That's all I want. I want you to say, 'This has been fun,' so I'll know."

Cash sat up and scooted back to lean against the tufted headboard of the bed. "You don't believe that I'm not going to ghost you, as you say."

"You always do, Cash. I'm not special. I'm just the next girl in line."

"I'm not the one who's going to leave," he said.

"Cash, I *know* you."

"I need to tell you something."

Her phone's screen winked off, and darkness folded around them. "We've been friends for three years. Anything that you haven't told me by now isn't important."

"Yes, it is. I don't talk about this."

"Do Arthur and Maxence know?"

"They saw the aftermath. No one else here knows about it."

A sound like Velcro ripping apart whispered through the dark.

"What did you do?" she asked.

"Our first time, out on the deck, we stayed out there in the dark because I had taken the bandage off my face before you came out. I couldn't find it to stick it back on. I couldn't walk through the lit house."

"Is the wound—" she chewed her tongue, searching for a non-stupid word, "—closed?"

"It's scarred over."

"Then it's just a scar."

"It's on my face."

"Yeah. So?"

"It's quite bad."

"I'm *quite* sure that I won't care."

"Someone as beautiful as you are will find it repulsive."

"I don't even know where to start with that. I *know* that I won't find you 'repulsive.' What a *horrible* word. A little scar is not going to chase me off."

"It's not little."

The air in the room began to gray. Outside, the horizon must be turning dark red and blue, the beginnings of sunrise.

His wooden blinds wouldn't keep out the sunlight. In just a few more minutes, she would be able to see what he meant.

"The scar doesn't matter." she said.

He paused, and Rox held her breath.

He finally said, "In the accident, glass went through my cheek, ripping skin and muscle. The surgeons couldn't do anything yet, but I'll have some work done on it soon."

"What kind of work?"

"Plastic surgery. Fillers. Dermabrasion. Laser resurfacing. It will reduce how visible it is."

Rox leaned toward him in the wisps of morning light. "It sounds like you know a lot about that."

He was silent for a moment in the quiet darkness. "Yes."

"You knew a lot about the work that Josie has had done, too."

A whisper in the air sounded like he had sighed. "Yes."

"Can you tell if I've had plastic surgery or not?"

A puff of air escaped his lips in a laugh. "If you have, it was done brilliantly. I think you were born absolutely beautiful."

She chuckled because she hadn't had any plastic surgery. "I'll bet you say that to all the girls."

Cash paused. A few streaks of light from the pale glimmerings of dawn touched the auburn in his hair and the point of his chin, but a strip of darkness lay across his cheek. "No, I don't."

"Of course you do."

"I don't. There's a lot that I don't say to anyone, that I've never said to anyone."

"Everybody does that, holds parts of themselves back or shows facets of themselves to certain groups, compartmentalizing." Sometimes, the twenty-dollar words came to her. "It's normal."

"This is different," he said. "There are things that happened to me when I was a child that I never told anyone."

He was a very private person, Arthur had said. "You don't have to tell me."

"I think I do." He sighed and looked at the wall across the room. "Yes, I need to tell you."

Pencil-thin lines of light rode across his face from the dawn's glimmerings shining through the horizontal slats, but she couldn't really see his face yet. "We've been friends for three years, and we've been okay with it this way."

He took both her hands in his and inhaled a deep breath. "When I was six, I was in a car accident."

"A car accident? Jesus, no wonder this accident freaked you out, even beyond the almost-dying part."

"The car that I was riding in flipped over the safety barrier and rolled down the side of a mountain.

"Oh, Lord." She gripped his hands more tightly in the dim light.

He said, "The seat belt didn't fit me right. I was too small. I went through the windshield."

She tightened her fingers around his. "Oh, God. *Cash.*"

"The glass scraped me up. I had cuts all over my body, crisscrossed, like I had gone through rollers of knives. Some were worse than others." He let go of her hand, and through the darkness, she could see his arm lift as he ran his fingers down the tattoo that covered his left shoulder and ribs under his tee shirt. "This side went through the window first. The tattoo is to hide the worst of the scars. Here. Feel."

He guided her fingers under the soft cotton of his shirt. His ribs were long lumps under his flesh, but the skin over them was rougher than the skin around the tattoo, thicker, like leather.

"The plastic surgeons sanded down the scars, so you can't feel much."

She ran her fingers over his skin, finding that odd texture under more of the tattoos. "Didn't that hurt?"

"A bit."

"Like sandblasting a few layers of your skin off?"

He shrugged. "That's pretty close."

"When you were *six?*"

"No. When I was eighteen and nineteen, during my undergraduate degree."

"Wow, Cash. I'm so sorry. At least it didn't mess up your face, huh?"

He held her other hand more tightly. "Actually, it did."

"They must have done an amazing job with the sandblaster."

"There weren't a lot of cuts on my face."

"Oh. Well, that's good."

"The bones inside were smashed. My cheekbones. My nose."

Rox covered her mouth with her hand.

"For most of elementary and high school, I was disfigured, rather badly. They couldn't do major reconstructive surgery until I had stopped growing." He lifted her fingers to his cheekbones, his jaw. "This is all plastic and cement. It's like I'm wearing a mask."

She ran her fingers over the hard lines of his cheekbones and jaw, trying to feel any seams or scars, but everything felt normal. "They did an amazing job. I can't feel anything that doesn't feel perfectly natural. Is this what you should have looked like?"

"It's probably close. They used pictures of my father when he was that age and of my younger brother Willem, who was seventeen at the time, to make the casts. They also did some age-progressed photos of me that had been taken before the accident, but I look more like my father, I think."

"I've never seen pictures of them. You don't have any pictures of them around."

"I've got some, somewhere. There's more than a familial resemblance."

His dry tone made her smile.

Early tendrils of sunlight leaked through the slats that covered the window.

In the dim light, something began to form on his cheek, something twisted.

Rox kept her hand cupped on his cheek on the other side of his face, the uninjured side. "Does the scar hurt now?"

"No."

Her fingers drifted around to the other side of his face. On his other cheek, hard lumps and pits puckered his skin. A crease and ridge ran under his cheekbone. "This feels like it must have hurt."

He shrugged. "It wasn't so bad. It was over with quickly."

The sunlight strengthened, and a dark rose glow infiltrated the blinds.

Under her fingers, gnarled skin marred Cash's cheek like wood knots growing under his skin in an area just below his cheekbone.

Even though she had felt it, seeing the damage on what had been perfection was shocking, like seeing someone slash a painting in a museum. "Oh, Cash."

His voice was quiet as he asked, "Are you going to leave?"

She glanced at the window. Scarlet light trickled though the blinds. "It's five in the morning."

"That's not what I meant."

She looked at him, startled. His green eyes

almost glowed with the red light staining his face. "I don't know what you're talking about."

He was watching her eyes very closely. "I mean, *me.* Are you going to leave *me?*"

Good Lord.

Heat flashed on her skin. "Do you actually mean, would I break up with you because you have a silly ol' scar on your face?"

Cash still didn't say anything. He just watched her, his emerald eyes wary in the brightening sunlight.

Righteous country anger began to simmer in her blood. "Are *you* saying that you *think* that I am so damn *shallow* that I would see a little scar on your face and take off for the *hills?*"

Confusion creased the skin between his eyebrows, and his lips opened.

Her voice hardened as the anger boiled up. "Casimir *Friso* van *Amsberg,* I have never been so *insulted* in all my life!"

His eyes widened. "I did not—"

She yanked her hands out of his and held them up by her shoulders, fingers splayed to strangle him. "You think that I am so *damn* superficial that I would give a *fig*—no, that I would give *a nit on a gnat's ass*—about that little *pucker* on your face and that I would walk out on you, that I would take my cats and *depart* as if you were a leper or an *atrocity.*"

He sputtered, "That's not what I—"

"That is *entirely* what you meant and you know it. You have a lot to learn about me, *Casimir Friso van*

Amsberg. I am not some fragile, inbred, hairless mutant cat who would keel over at the sight of blood or a bit of scar tissue. That is *ridiculous.*"

The corners of his mouth rose just a little, and he turned his chin to look at her out of the corners of his eyes. "I'll have to make you angry more often."

"Oh, I don't think that's a good idea at all, *Casimir.* I will whup your effete Euro *butt* if you say something like that to me *ever* again."

His smile curved more. "I like it when you say my name."

"I say your name all the time. I've yelled it across the office and screamed it at the ceiling once or twice, too."

"Casimir. You're calling me *Casimir.*"

"That's right. I am angry enough to call you by your full and legal name. You had best *beware.*"

He blinked, looking at her face. "I like it when you call me Casimir."

"Well, that's neither here nor there. I am so irritated with you that I could spit."

He stroked her arm, his smile warming. "If all this has persuaded you to call me Casimir instead of Cash, then it was worth it."

"I declare, I will go get a horsewhip if you do not stop provoking me."

"You do have a temper, don't you, *lieveke?*"

"Oh, you have no idea. Once I get riled up, I *stay* riled up. Watch out when I go *biblical,* and let me assure you, I am nearly *there.*"

He wrapped his arms around her, pressing his whole body against hers. The heat from his flesh warmed her long tee shirt and her skin underneath, and he kissed the tender spot where her neck met her shoulder. “I won’t bring it up again.”

“That’s the first sensible thing you’ve said all morning.”

He chuckled against her skin and held her more closely. “I want you to come to Amsterdam with me next weekend.”

So this was it, the start of the whirlwind-travel phase of their relationship, where they jetted off to Europe for no good reason.

At least it meant that he wasn’t ghosting on her just yet.

She asked, “Why Amsterdam?”

“There are some people whom I want you to meet.”

“Your sister, Ana?”

“Among others.”

“It would be nice to meet her.” Ana had known to send Maxence and Arthur, the perfect foils for Cash’s downward spiral. Rox should thank her and tell her that it had worked.

Maybe she should bake Ana some brownies or something.

“She’ll love you,” Cash whispered.

“She seems nice. I’m sure I’ll just love her, too.”

Cash rested his forehead on the side of her head, his lips near her ear, and he whispered, “I love you.”

Rox's throat collapsed. She couldn't speak or breathe.

Wren had said that he wasn't lovey-dovey. On Rox's first day, Melanie had said that Cash wasn't mushy and didn't lie about what was going on.

Rox closed her eyes and just felt his strong arms around her.

God, she wanted so much to believe him.

An echo of his words jumped around inside her, a vibration straining to get out, but her throat was constricted so tightly that she could only sip air. She couldn't speak. She couldn't *think.*

"And I don't say that to all the other girls," Cash said. "I haven't said that to anyone except you. I've been in love with you for years, torn between wanting you to divorce Grant and yet not wanting you to suffer through a divorce."

This didn't compute. This was contrary to all the laws of the state and nature. Cash Amsberg didn't fall in love with anyone. He just fucked his way through the office contact list and client roster.

Rox carefully, slowly, slipped her arms around his waist, trying to tell him with her body because her throat would not open.

"I've wanted to tell you this for so long, that I love you. I've wanted you in my arms, in my bed, in my life *this* way, not just at work. I won't ghost on you. I've been waiting for you for so long."

Rox turned in his arms and buried her face against his chest, holding him as hard as she could.

Even with his splenectomy scar right under her

arm, he wasn't in any danger of being hurt by her squeezing him. She wasn't strong enough to hurt him.

She was too weak, far too weak where he was concerned. She wanted to believe him so much.

"I love you, too," she whispered. "Don't ghost on me. No matter what. I couldn't bear it now."

His arms tightened around her, and his fingers wove into her hair. He curled around her, protecting her, holding her in his arms and with his whole body. "I won't ghost on you. I won't leave you, ever."

"Don't get creepy," she said, her voice choked because she didn't want to cry but she couldn't quite laugh.

He chuckled. "I won't get creepy, but I love you and I won't leave you, *lieveke.*"

They sat that way for a few more moments until it seemed prudent to lie down before they fell over, and they slept in each others' arms in the morning sunlight for another hour.

Chapter Sixty-Three

PRINCE MONSTER

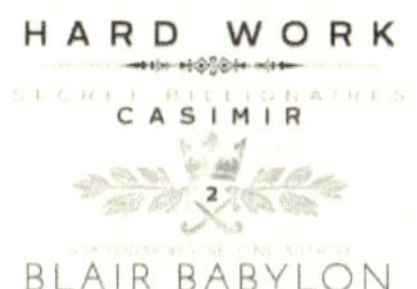

Rox wandered out of Cash's bedroom to go to the kitchen to rustle up some breakfast.

Cash had left his bedroom a few minutes before her, kissing her on the forehead and then ducking to kiss her on the lips before he went out to make sure that Arthur and Maxence had found food and coffee.

As Rox closed the bedroom door behind her to walk down the hallway, Maxence turned the corner from some guest bedroom in the deeper part of the house and smiled at her.

She lifted her chin and refused to be shamed by the wannabe priest catching her leaving a man's bedroom in the morning. Hey, Maxence had definitely followed that black leather-clad woman out of the office at The Devilhouse, and from what Arthur had said, he wasn't as pure as Irish butter before that, either.

He was following her down the hallway, however. She should probably wait and walk with him to be polite. She leaned against the wall, crossing her arms over her chest.

Maxence was wearing another tailored black suit, bringing to mind priests, morticians, and ravens. It fit his broad shoulders and tapered to his athletic waist and long legs too well to have been bought off the rack, and the discreet stylishness of it caught even Rox's attention.

Talk about mixed messages.

While she leaned against the wall, waiting, Maxence was inspecting the art hanging on the long hallway's walls as he strolled, his hands clasped behind his back. He hadn't seen that she was hanging out, waiting for him.

A lot of art hung on the walls of Cash's house.

Rox stared at the painting across from her of a still life of fruit, glowing scarlets and oranges. She drifted over to look at a landscape painting of a Spanish fort on a hillside. Another painting farther down the hall was of an archway, draped with ivy and flowering vines.

None of the paintings were portraits of people.

Cash didn't have any mirrors in his bedroom or the common areas, either.

Or pictures of his sister or other family.

No *faces,* at all.

Her heart broke a little more for him.

Maxence was close enough to talk to without yelling down the hallway.

She said, "I need to talk to you."

Maxence walked to meet her in the hallway. "All right."

"So you're His Holiness Pope Fuckitall."

He folded his hands behind his back and smiled, looking down at his feet. "That's a rather recent nickname. As a child, I was the Emperor Maximum. I grew to my adult height about six months before everyone started to grow in eighth standard."

Rox pressed, "And Arthur is the Earl of Givesnofucks."

"He's always had that nickname. You can see why."

"So what was Cash?"

Maxence lifted his head and looked down at her, a wariness in his dark eyes. "How much has he told you about his childhood?"

"He told me that he was in a horrific car accident that smashed his face, but he didn't have reconstructive surgery until he was eighteen."

"Ah." Maxence's shoulders dropped about two inches, and he blinked slowly. "Good. He's a very private person in some ways."

"So what did you guys call him?"

His eyebrows twitched downward, and he sighed. "We didn't give him the name. He insisted that Arthur and I call him that. He owned it, and he wore it like a mantle to throw it back at people who tormented him."

Rox's hands curled into fists at the thought of someone tormenting Cash. "He was a kid."

"Children can be cruel." He actually flinched as he looked at the walls. "Certain children, especially, seemed to be born with no conscience. Casimir's treatment at the hands of certain people is what made me study theodicy, why evil exists in the world. Arthur and I tried to protect Casimir from those kinds of people, but he wouldn't allow it."

Rox shook her head. "Yeah, he wouldn't."

"He always battles injustice, and he won't let other people fight his battles for him. Most of the boys were fine. After they got to know him, everybody liked him. Heart of gold and all that. Always picked for teams early, too."

"All the guys love him at the office."

"That's Casimir. Everyone's a friend. No one could have actually teased him even if we had wanted to. None of the boys, anyway."

A few tumblers fell into place on the lock that was Cash Amsberg. Rox clarified, "None of the boys, you said."

He nodded. "None of the boys."

"But the girls?"

Maxence studied a painting of a golden bowl full of jewel-toned fruit. "The girls were different. When we were very young, it wasn't a problem. Once everyone hit puberty, though, things changed for him. There was some groupthink going on, not uncommon in children."

"I'm not sure I want to know this anymore."

"I think you should." He still wouldn't look at her, though.

"Okay." She took a deep breath and steeled herself.

Maxence pursed his lips. "They toyed with him."

"This sounds really bad."

He nodded. "They dared each other to go out with him, to kiss him, to make him fall in love with them, and then they laughed at him to his face and among their friends. It was brutal. No one could stop him from believing them and falling in love with them, until one day, he didn't anymore."

"Oh."

"Something clicked in him, and he never believed them after that day. When one of them approached him, he was unflaggingly polite, but his eyes were hollow for hours afterward. We watched him to make sure that he didn't ski into a tree or stop swimming in the middle of the lake."

She looked at the Spanish tile under her feet. "Okay."

Maxence nodded, biting his lower lip.

Rox planted her hands on her hips so that Maxence wouldn't see them shake. "So what did you guys call him?"

Maxence stared at his feet, embarrassed. His mouth went tight, and he enunciated very precisely, "Prince Monster."

Chapter Sixty-Four

ARTHUR'S WORK HERE IS DONE

HARD WORK
CASIMIR
BLAIR BABYLON

In the kitchen, Cash was sitting at the table by the front window with Arthur. Empty cereal bowls stood on the table between them.

Cash was holding his spoon in his hand, pointing it at Arthur's nose like he was going to shank him.

Arthur was inspecting the tip of the spoon as if something was clinging to it.

Both looked up when Rox came in, then looked over her shoulder when Maxence walked in behind her.

Arthur asked, "Are you packed?"

Rox asked, "For what?" but behind her, Maxence said, "Yes. We can leave whenever you want."

"Where are you off to now?" Cash asked.

"Home," Arthur said. "I have socialized all the kittens in Los Angeles, and so my work here is done."

Cash raised an eyebrow. "More like you managed to coax Maxence and me into going to The Devilhouse with you, so you've tempted us enough with your evil ways."

Arthur pretended to frown. "Evil lurks only in the hearts of men, not in our dicks. Support me here, Maxence."

"I'm not getting involved in this conversation." Maxence's breezy tone didn't seem serious, but it did sound like he had heard that line of reasoning far too often.

Or maybe he just feared for his immortal soul whenever Arthur was around. Rox wondered just how often Arthur felt the need to tempt Maxence, whether with liquor or women or who knew what else Arthur was into. She wandered over to the cabinets and poured herself a bowl of cereal.

"Fine, don't support my position." Arthur's dry drawl suggested that he didn't believe Maxence for one minute. "But you would still like a lift to London, wouldn't you?"

Maxence shrugged. "If you wouldn't mind."

Arthur's grin and the squint of his silvery eyes bordered on demonic. "It would be my pleasure."

Chapter Sixty-Five

SUB MODO

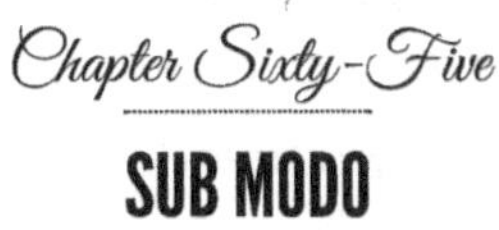

Rox strode through the law firm from her office toward Cash's, careful to skirt the long way around the cubicle farm to avoid Val's and Josie's offices.

Wren discreetly waved at her over the top of her padded walls, but a lot of the other paralegals kept their heads down and their gazes, averted. The mumble and mutter of the office died down as she walked through.

She holed up in her own office for a few minutes before she met with Cash in his. Flipping through the document security system just pissed her off more. Josie and Val had been into everything, all of Cash's contracts, everything that Rox had worked on, and a bunch of other contracts, too. Obviously, they had been searching for something or trying to hide what they had done.

She skulked around the perimeter of the cubicle farm to get to Cash's office. Something was definitely going on, and the rabble knew about it. If she asked someone, though, she might get them into trouble.

Cash opened his office door for her. "Meeting time?"

"Eleven," Rox said. "We've got half an hour. Cash, do you want to look at the DiCaprio contract?"

"Casimir," he said, shutting the door behind her.

Rox looked behind herself. "Pardon me?"

He closed the distance between them and folded her into his arms. *"Casimir,* not Cash. I've never liked that nickname. You started calling me Casimir this morning. Don't stop."

"I, well, okay. I might slip sometimes, Casimir," she said, trying it out. It sounded funny, but it fit him. Calling him by his whole, real name was a little more exotic, a little more formal, and yet intimate.

"That's all right." He kissed the top of her head. "Do you want me to call you Roxanne?"

"Ain't nobody but my daddy called me by my full name, and then only when he was threatening to whup my butt for being sassy."

"I did not understand a word that you said, but I'll assume that I'm to continue calling you Rox."

"You're not wrong."

He laughed and released her. "Pull up the revised draft for that DiCaprio contract. It should've come in last night."

Rox pulled her computer out of her purse and logged on. "Yep, there it is."

Cash moved around behind her to look at the screen. He braced his arms on the desk, one on each side of her, something that he wouldn't have done a month ago. He rested his chin on her shoulder. "Go to the compensation section, Twelve Point Six."

Rox skimmed the solid black blocks of text on the screen. "Casimir," she said carefully, "this says 'net' again. They changed it back. They're trying to give DiCaprio a share of the *net* profits instead of the gross."

"What? It *can't.* We changed that in the document while we were sitting in the conference room. Are you sure that's the right file?"

"It was the last file on the list, the most recent." She flipped back to the screen that listed all the documents. "Yep, look. It came in at eleven-thirty last night."

"So they changed it *back?* Why would they do that?"

"I have no idea, and the note on the side says that it was *sub modo.*"

"We certainly didn't agree to that," Cash mused.

Cash? Casimir. Yeah, Casimir.

She asked, "But why would they tag it as *sub modo?* That's insane. It's like they wanted us to catch it."

"Or they didn't take care because they assumed that no one would ever look at it. It's possible that the agents have been conspiring to screw their clients, and we've been wrongly accusing Val and Josie of malpractice."

"I would be dang hard-pressed to believe that it was *all* of the agents, *every single one of them,*" Rox said. "And besides, they make a percentage of their clients' fees. They have no reason to reduce what their clients are paid."

Casimir scratched his cheek and squinted at the ceiling, thinking.

"Let me check something." Her fingers rattled over the keyboard. "No, all of these contracts are from different agents and even different agencies. If the agents are the guilty ones, then they're all psychic because they're all doing *exactly* the same thing, *exactly* at the same time, in *exactly* the same way."

Casimir frowned. "That's unlikely."

"Statistically impossible," she agreed.

"Can't the document security system tell us who checked things out?"

"Yeah, I think it can." Rox tapped a bunch of keys, searching the list.

There should have been a list of people who had dropped the contract in the cloud, but that list was empty except for Rox's name. A hot flash of panic puffed over her at seeing only her own name, even though she knew that she hadn't done anything wrong.

And of course her name was on that list. She had dropped it into the cloud so that they could work on it at Cash's house.

However, there was a list of people who had accessed the contract from inside the office, too.

The first name on the list was Wren Sishi.

Wren's name peppered the list. *Weird.* She must have been getting someone other than Rox to log her on.

Even the last name on the list was Wren Sishi, and she had supposedly edited it at six o'clock that morning.

Wren? At the office at six o'clock in the godforsaken morning?

Unlikely.

Rox pointed to Wren's name on the screen. "That can't be right. Wren is *never* here that early. She's never *anywhere* that early. She rushes in late at nine-thirty every day."

"Maybe if someone paid her well enough," Casimir said.

"And she's hopeless at using the tokens to log onto the system. She always needs help. You remember a couple months ago when I got an emergency text in the meeting with Lourde Clinchy's people? Wren was freaking because she couldn't log onto the system, and she was too embarrassed to tell anyone else. I had to leave the meeting to help her."

"Maybe it was a ruse to make people think that it wasn't her."

"Then it was a very long and embarrassing and perfectly consistent *ruse.*" *A ruse.* Man, he sounded British sometimes.

Cash's breath was warm on her neck. *Casimir's breath.* He said, "Good. We need to talk to her. Tell her that we have a few questions about some other contract and bring her in."

He pushed himself away from the desk so that Rox could leave, but she was sure that his hand grazed her hip, his fingers lingering on her skirt.

Rox wanted to turn and grab him, hold him and hear him whisper in her ear again, but she swallowed hard and walked out of his office door.

She trotted through the cubicle farm to Wren's desk. "Hey, can you come talk with us for a sec?"

"Yeah, sure." Wren followed her, but she kept looking around nervously, her blond hair swishing around her shoulders as she walked.

Back in the office, the three of them sat down on the couches around the coffee table. Cash's law school diploma hung high on the wall above them.

Cash was leaning back, his arms resting on the back of the couch. Rox sat on the opposite end of the couch from him, trying to make it look like they weren't screwing around.

Wren was hunched forward, her arms crossed and her elbows resting on her knees. "Val and Josie called us all into a meeting first thing this morning. They said that some irregularities have been found in the contracts, and they're bringing in an outside firm to investigate what has been going on. So, you must have told them what you found?"

"In a manner of speaking," Cash said.

"What time was the meeting?" Rox asked.

Wren rolled her eyes. "Right at nine."

"Did you make it in time?"

Wren laughed, but the harsh sound was more like a nervous cackle. "I skated in and stood in the back for part of it."

So Wren couldn't have opened the DiCaprio contract at six in the morning in the office, assuming that she was telling the truth about when she had dragged herself into the office.

"You sure about the time?" Rox asked her.

Wren squinted at her. "Yeah. I had trouble catching on to what they were talking about. Something about the security system and how no one knows what's been checked out or hasn't been or what's going on."

"Well, we know what's been going on," Rox said, crossing her knees. "We just don't know *how.*"

"Or why," Cash said. "The studios' motivation is obviously money, but I am shocked that Val would be a part of this."

Wren shook her head. "But Val wouldn't have done it. She just wouldn't have. Do you think it could be Josie?"

"Why do you think Val didn't do it?" Cash asked.

"I just can't imagine her doing anything like that. She's always been so strict about everything ethical."

Rox shrugged. "Might be Val. Might be Josie. Might be both of them."

Casimir turned toward her on the couch. "Oh?"

"A couple weeks ago, Josie gaslighted me."

Cash raised one eyebrow. "And that means?"

Rox spread her empty hands in front of her. "I mentioned to her that we had found some irregularities in Val's contracts, some clauses that were detrimental to our clients, and she told me that either I was imagining it or that you were lying about it, or you were mistaken. She made me feel like I was crazy. She said that she didn't trust a junior partner's opinion over Valerie's, and she kind of threatened my job."

Cash's jaw set in a harder line. "I wouldn't have thought that of Josie."

"I wouldn't have, either." Rox turned to Wren. "What else happened at that meeting?"

Wren crunched down farther, almost hugging her knees. "They said that we should cooperate fully with the investigators and that we shouldn't talk to anyone else who might be asking questions, especially anybody else in the office. They said that anyone asking questions and anyone answering questions for anyone but the investigators would be let go." She looked up, her short eyelashes nearly touching the epicanthic fold of her eyelids. "I think she meant you two."

Casimir looked over at Rox and exhaled hard. "Wren, go back to your desk. If anyone asks what we talked about, tell them that you were asking about this scar on my cheek." He pointed to the small patch of gnarled skin below his cheekbone. "Glass went through my face in the accident."

Rox flinched and tried to send psychic messages to Wren to not make a big deal about it.

"Oh." Wren squinted at him. "I guess you do have a scar there."

He blinked. "Yes."

"If you grow your beard back out a little, no one will be able to see it at all." She smiled at him. "You always looked good with a little scruff. Kind of lumbersexual, except that I can't imagine you in a plaid shirt."

"I'll take that under consideration," he said.

"Okay. That's what I'll tell people." Relief lightened Wren's voice.

"Go now," Cash told her, "before you're in here too long."

Casimir, Rox reminded herself. *Not Cash. Casimir.* Jeez, this was not going to be easy.

Wren practically fled the office, her light steps silent on the carpeting. The door clicked shut behind her.

Rox looked down at her hands, twisting in her lap. "So we really can't talk to anyone else, either."

"No. It's almost time for my meeting with Val anyway," Cash said.

Rox frowned at him. "What do you mean *my* meeting? I'm going in with you."

"No, you're not. If this goes badly, I don't want you to lose your job, too."

"Yeah, you might end up living with me and the cats in a one-bedroom apartment."

"You don't have one of those."

She smirked at him. "I will totally get one just to see you try to fit in it."

He laughed. "Don't forget that we're going to Amsterdam this weekend, no matter what. If we both lose our jobs, maybe we'll just stay in Europe."

Rox rolled her eyes. "I don't *think* so, buddy. It took me my whole life to get to California. I'm not giving up the beach and the sunshine that easily."

"The Netherlands is right on the ocean. Scheveningen has a very nice beach, and there's a beach area even within the city of Amsterdam."

"I thought Holland was below sea level, and that's why you have those dikes and windmills and stuff."

"We still have beaches."

"You didn't say anything about sunshine," she pointed out.

He shrugged. "Sometimes we have sunshine. The weather is notoriously variable."

"Great. *Variable.*"

"With luck, the weather should still be nice enough that we could sit on the beach this weekend. Pack a bathing suit."

Rox snorted at him. "I will. A beach below sea level. This, I have to see."

Chapter Sixty-Six

AMSBERG V. ARBEITMAN, ROUND THREE

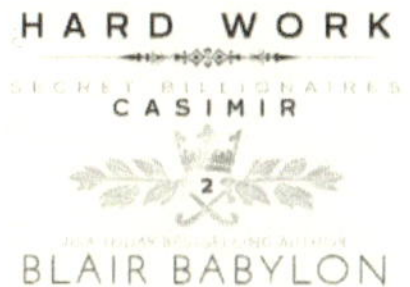

Rox's heavy purse, slung over her shoulder, bounced against her back as she strode toward Valerie Arbeitman's office. Cash walked beside her, his long legs covering the ground so that she had to trot to keep up.

Casimir, dang it. Not Cash. This was definitely going to take some getting used to.

He carried his briefcase and a few pages that they had printed out from the DiCaprio contract with the damning language in it.

When they passed Wren's desk, she didn't even look up at them. Her blonde hair hung like a curtain around her face.

They dodged through the cubicles like a maze, and no one met their eyes. Everyone seemed to be very busy looking at whatever was on their computer screens or their desks or their laps or their feet.

Rox hurried to keep up with Cash. Usually, he was good about waiting for her while she trotted beside him, but when he was riled up, those long legs of his stretched even longer, she could just swear.

At Valerie's door, Cash stopped and looked back, waiting, with his fist raised to knock.

"I'm here," Rox said, a little breathless from walking so fast.

He bent down and whispered to her, "If this goes badly, switch sides. Don't get fired."

"I'm not going to hang you out to dry."

"Almost certainly, I'm going to need to take this to the state ethics board. I may need you in here to get documents for me."

"I don't like that at all, Casimir." Hey, she got it right that time. "I don't want to work someplace where this kind of thing is going on."

He knocked on the door. "If she threatens to fire me, I'm telling you to switch sides. Indeed, don't say anything until we see how this is going to play out."

From inside the office, a woman's voice called, "Come in."

Casimir opened the door.

Inside the office, both Valerie and Josie stood around Val's desk, waiting for them to come in. Rox could see that both senior partners were wearing their resting bitch faces as if they were going into court for a tough hearing.

Uh oh.

Val said, "Come in. We need to talk to both of you."

Evidently, it was already too late for Rox to

switch sides, anyway. She trudged in after Cash and took a chair.

Casimir remained standing and slapped the pages from the DiCaprio contract on Val's desk. "What is the meaning of this?"

Val glanced down at the pages but didn't pick them up to read them. "It doesn't matter what those are. You have been interrogating the paralegals and admins about what you call the 'irregularities' in the contracts that the agents submit to us. This is in violation of law firm policy."

"What you are doing is in 'violation' of every ethical standard. If this does not stop immediately, I will have to report this to the state ethics board. All previous contracts must also be amended to make them ethical."

She wanted to stand up and cheer. *You go get them, Cash.*

No.

Wait.

Casimir.

You go get them, Casimir.

Yeah, that was it.

Val said, "Ms. Silverman and I are in agreement. We are terminating your partnership with this law firm, Cash."

He leaned over the desk at them. "You're only pushing me out to cover up what you're doing."

Val's voice rose. "We will buy you out at the previously agreed-upon price. Effective immediately, you are no longer employed at this firm and need to leave the premises immediately."

"This is unethical. It's illegal. I will make sure that they disbar you."

"They won't take *my* license. They may disbar *you.*"

"You have been swindling clients."

"Who do you think they will believe, a junior partner who has only been here for a few years, or *me,* a senior partner who has worked in this industry for decades? I know most of the people on the state ethics board. I went to law school with three of them and have slept with two of the others. Plus, we have ample evidence that you and Ms. Neil here have been swindling clients at the behest of the studios for years."

"Me?" Rox grabbed the arms of the chair. "I don't even have the authority to make changes in the documents. I can make notes but not changes."

When Val looked at her, the attorney's brown eyes were cold and dark. "You have been checking out the documents for Cash to modify. You've been using Wren's identification codes to smuggle the documents out so that we wouldn't know that it was you. You may have also been using Cash's login to change them yourself."

"I don't even know—" But of course, Rox did know Wren's login codes and Cash's, too. She had helped Wren log into the document control system so many times because she was hopeless at it. Rox did stuff for Cash in his documents all the time, too.

Damn.

Val was still staring at her. "And when you drop them in the cloud, suddenly the words change to our clients' detriment."

"That's not right," she said. "We haven't touched DiCaprio's contract since the meeting with his attorneys. They sent over the new draft last night. But the wording was changed at six o'clock this morning. It had to have been done by someone who was in the office, and we didn't get here until after ten."

"I think you did it," Val said. "I think you came in and logged in as Wren this morning. She never gets here before nine, so it must have been you. I think you two changed all the contracts."

Casimir said, "We did not have access or editing authority on your contracts after you came back from your leave of absence, but your contracts were the ones with the clauses that swindled our clients."

"And yet," Josie chimed in, "we think you did it, and I'll bet that as soon as we fire you, we will stop discovering these problem clauses."

Rox didn't like the way that she had said that at all. Yeah, they would stop *discovering* the problems, all right. "We didn't do it."

Val said, "And we think you did, and we both are in agreement that you need to leave the premises now. Do not stop at your desks. Do not speak to anyone. Security should be waiting for you outside my door to escort you out of the building."

Indignation drove Rox to her feet. "Are you

kidding me? You're having the security guards throw us out of the building?"

"Immediately," Josie said. The angry set of her jaw infuriated Rox.

"I want my rubber plant," Rox said. "I grew that plant from a little six-inch wilting sapling that Melanie couldn't keep alive. I want my plant."

Cash glanced back at her, his green eyes squinting with disbelief, but he didn't say anything.

Val threw her hands in the air. "Fine. You can go get your plant, but that's all."

"It's a big plant," Casimir said, "and it's in a heavy pot. She can't carry it. I need to carry it for her."

"Fine. Go with her and get her damn plant, but the security guys are going with you. Don't give us a reason to add assault charges to anything that we have to tell the ethics board."

Casimir stepped to the side, and Rox walked out of Val's office ahead of him. Two security guys were waiting outside of Val's door, and they both trailed Rox and Casimir to her office.

Rox walked straight in her own office door, and when Casimir stopped in the doorway and held his arms up to lean on the doorjamb, she swiped a thumb drive-sized thing that was sitting on her desk and palmed it, holding it against her leg so that no one could see she had anything there.

Her huge rubber plant was still standing against the window right where she had left it, its leaves spread against the glass, blocking the view of the security guy who tried to look around it.

"Hey!" the guy said. "You aren't taking anything right?"

"Nope," Rox called back to him and grabbed her favorite mug. "Nothing important, anyway."

The cup read *Work Wife.* Casimir had given it to her a few months before with a nice little bouquet stuck in it.

Yeah, she did want to take the mug with her.

Casimir set his briefcase on the carpet by the pot, and he stooped and grabbed the plant's heavy clay container.

"Wait," she said. "Are you sure you should be lifting that?"

"I'm fine," he said. "I can carry this. I've carried —" he glanced at the two security guys, "—heavier things than this."

"I don't want you to hurt yourself. You know what? The plant isn't worth it. We'll just leave it here for whomever gets the office."

The security guy on the left crossed his arms and sighed. "We need to escort you two out of the building."

"Come on," she said, picking up her heavy purse and slinging it across her back again. "Let's get out of here."

As they crossed the lobby, Melanie ran up to them, holding a manila envelope. "Cash! Rox!" She shoved the envelope into Rox's hands.

Rox looked at the envelope, but nothing was written on it. "What's this?"

"The settlement offer from the apartment property management company." Melanie glanced behind herself like she expected assassins to jump out and grab her. "I've got things to do." She scuttled away.

Rox pulled the documents out and scanned them.

The number written in the first paragraph had a lot of zeroes in it.

A lot of them.

A key slithered out of the envelope and plunked on the carpet at her feet.

She said, "Holy cow! I just wanted my stuff and my deposit back."

Casimir snagged the key from the floor near her feet and took her elbow to guide her away. "We should go. The security gentlemen are getting nervous."

Indeed, they were fidgeting with their walkie-talkies, as if the static-crackling communication devices would coerce Rox. "This is enough money to *buy* a house."

"It's illegal to put a device on someone's door without going through the proper eviction procedures, which take months. I pointed that out, including sending pictures of the device and the proper statutes, and the property management company became unnerved, offering settlements. I negotiated a nice settlement for you in exchange for not turning the documents over to the D.A. The key is to a storage unit with your other property in it."

Rox stared at the enormous sum again. "You blackmailed them?"

Not that she was particularly sorry about it. They were going to lock her out without her cats and do God-knew-what to her cats.

Casimir shrugged. "It's not blackmail if a lawyer does it on behalf of a client. Then, it's *negotiation.*"

Chapter Sixty-Seven

SHOTS FIRED

Rox drove on the crowded freeways while Casimir sat in the passenger seat, fuming. Traffic flowed and eddied around them, a rushing river of cars that Rox navigated, slipping from one lane to another.

Casimir said, "Why would Val and Josie do such a thing? Now, I am absolutely going to the state ethics board as soon as I can prepare the case. If they hadn't fired me, I probably would've continued to try to resolve the problems from within the law office."

"Yeah, they really gave us the bum's rush out of there." Jitters ran through her at the thought of losing her job, coupled with the huge settlement from the apartment's management company.

Too much adrenaline.

She glanced at the hills that rose on both sides of the freeway. Golden autumn weeds rippled on the steep slopes. If someone sideswiped them here, at least they wouldn't roll down an embankment. Ever since Casimir had told her about the car crash that he had been in when he was a kid, she had been imagining every flip of the car and the sickening shrieks of twisting metal punching into his little-boy body. She tightened her fists around the steering wheel.

Casimir asked her, "So why did you steal the token?"

Rox shrugged. "Just to piss them off. Josie goes nuts when one of them is missing. Those two assholes will hunt for hours for it before they go home tonight."

He laughed. "We don't need to get in there, do we? My laptop has a bunch of contracts on it, and it is at home. You carried your laptop out in your purse. We should have all the evidence that we need to put our case together for the ethics board. They should have ample evidence to decide whether or not to censure them, disbar them, or file charges against them."

"I just don't care. I hate that we got fired when they're the guilty ones. So I swiped it. Just to be a big ol' bitch."

Crack, a bang slapped Rox's ears.

The windshield spiderwebbed and split.

"Good Lord, that truck must have thrown a huge rock," she said.

The explosion of cracks in the windshield cut the road into a thousand pieces. Afternoon sunlight glowed in the cracks, making the spiderweb catch fire.

Rox squinted to see through the broken windshield and looked back to check the SUV's blind spot before she pulled over.

Casimir said, "Don't pull over. Keep driving."

"I can't see much of anything through the cracks." The car to their right had drifted back, so Rox changed lanes to get to the shoulder of the road. She pulled into the emergency lane and braked hard, stopping the SUV.

As they stopped, Cash's window shattered inward, spraying them both with broken glass.

"Gunshot. They're shooting at us." He grabbed her neck, shoved her down on the seat, and crawled over her, shielding her with his body. "Push the accelerator with your foot. Now. *Hard.*"

Rox kicked the accelerator pedal, and the SUV lurched forward. Her cheek was pressed against the leather upholstery, and Cash's jacket flapped in front of her face. The seatbelt bit into her shoulder.

Cash said, "Release the catch on my seatbelt. I can't reach it."

Rox extended her fingers above her hair and found the buckle and the button to pop his seatbelt. She squeezed it, and Cash leaned on her a little more heavily. He laid on top of her, hunched over and peeking above the dash while he drove with one hand.

The emergency brake handle between the bucket seats was bruising her ribs, but she stayed mashed flat to the seats, trying to not move under Casimir so he could drive the SUV.

Another pop crashed through the SUV. Broken glass shot through the air, flipping over the back of the seat and peppering her back.

Rox wrapped her arms around Casimir's waist, trying to steady both of them. If the car flipped now, he would fly out the broken front windshield.

"Faster," Cash said. "More gas."

She hesitated.

More gas meant more acceleration, more speed if they hit something and flipped.

He would fly out the window. She couldn't hold him.

Another bullet slammed into the car. More glass showered them.

"Now!"

Rox shoved her foot down.

The engine snarled.

The SUV leapt forward.

"Come on, come on," Casimir muttered. He twisted the steering wheel, turning off on an exit. "Brake now."

Rox stomped on the brake. The SUV's tires screeched under them. They slid, and they stopped.

Casimir said, "Stay down."

He moved up a little bit, looking around, and Rox sucked in a deep breath of air when his weight lightened. She asked, "Are we okay?"

A crack, and a clang rang through the car, metal on metal.

"No," Casimir said. "Gas."

Rox stepped on the gas pedal, and Cash drove them through the streets, muttering directions to her. It was a miracle they didn't hit anybody, but after a few minutes, Cash told her to brake one more time. The gear shift handle beside her waist moved, and the SUV flinched as the engine shifted into the parking gear.

Casimir said, "I think we lost him."

"What the hell was that?" Rox asked, still clinging to his waist.

He sat up, maneuvering himself back to the passenger seat, though he still had one hand on the steering wheel and was looking around. "I think that sniper was the reason why Val needed us to get out of the office so fast. I am reconsidering my position that my car crash was just an accident."

"No shit, Sherlock!" Rox shoved at Casimir to get him off of her and pushed herself up on her arms. "I can't believe that Val is trying to kill you over this!"

"I'm not sure it's Val," he said, grabbing the door handle to pull himself upright. "I think she tried to warn me. When I argued with her earlier this week, she kept telling me that I didn't understand, to back off, and to make sure that you had no part in it. I think Val and Josie are either being threatened or blackmailed." He looked at the shattered windows. "Probably threatened."

A police car pulled up alongside of them, its siren wailing and lights glaring in their eyes. The officer shoved open her door and jumped out to crouch behind her car, her gun pointing over the car's roof at Rox and Casimir. She yelled, "Get out of the car!"

"Whoa!" Rox poked the button to roll down the driver's side window and held up her empty hands. "We were shot at. We don't have any guns, and we didn't do anything wrong."

The officer lifted her head so that she was not peering over the gun's sights. She looked them over, the sun shining off the polished brim of her hat as her head dipped. "Someone just started shooting at you?"

From behind Rox, Casimir said, "There was a sniper. How many cars did he shoot at?"

"Looked like a couple cars were hit. Are you folks okay?" she called across the top of the car.

"Yeah," Rox said. "I think so. A little shaken up."

"I'll bet." The officer holstered her gun and walked around her car toward them, though her fingers hovered near her weapon. "Do you need an ambulance or other medical attention?"

Casimir said, "I think we're all right."

The officer walked over to Rox's door. "Can I see some identification?"

"I'm going to take my wallet out of my pocket," Casimir said, his hands still raised.

"Yes, sir," the officer said, her fingers lightly touching the butt of her gun.

"And I'm going to dig around in my purse for a minute," Rox said. "It's kind of a mess in there."

"Yes, ma'am." The officer's shoulders had relaxed, and Rox turned away to root through her purse for her billfold.

Casimir passed his driver's license to the officer over Rox's shoulder. "I have additional identification and the rental agreement for the SUV in my briefcase. There are just a few other pieces of paper in there, a laptop, and so on."

"Sure," the officer said. "Move slowly, if you wouldn't mind."

"Of course, madam." He slid his fingertips into a side pocket of the briefcase and took out a small, thin book with a burgundy and gold cover. The lions stamped on the front kind of looked like Casimir's tattoo on the inside of his forearm.

The officer reached for it over Rox's shoulder again, while Rox was still stirring the boxes of mints and gum and tissue and tampons and receipts, trying to dig up her wallet. She got a glimpse of the cover of Casimir's passport as they passed it right by her face. The words on the front read, *Diplomatiek Paspoort.*

Those words might have been Dutch, but Rox could figure out what they meant. She was still so shocked-stupid from getting shot at and nearly dying on the freeway that she almost giggled at the fact that his official diplomatic passport had the word "poo" in it.

Rox found her thick wallet in her purse and

unzipped it on three sides. Damn, she had meant to clean it out. The wallet was so full that it looked like she had stuffed a deck of playing cards in there.

"It's here." Rox glanced back at the police officer while she separated the loyalty rewards cards and credit cards and gym ID with her fingernails. "I swear to God, it's in here."

"Take your time." The officer examined the small book and asked Casimir, "Is this real?"

"Yes, ma'am," he said.

"We don't see this kind of thing very often."

Casimir shrugged. "I can call someone, if you'd prefer."

"It's no problem. I just have to check it out."

Among the cluster of cards in her wallet, Rox found her driver's license. She put her thumb over the picture lest Casimir see that horrible photo and held it out to the police officer. "Found it."

"Thank you, ma'am. I'll just run these." The officer walked back to her car and bent to get in the front seat.

"What was that?" Rox asked.

Cash raised one eyebrow. "What?"

"That passport. That diplomatic passport."

"I carry a diplomatic passport. It gets me out of parking tickets."

"This isn't a parking ticket."

"And we didn't do anything wrong. We were the victims of a crime, and the passport will help smooth things over."

"Why does a lawyer need a diplomatic

passport?"

He was looking straight at her, and while he didn't look angry, he did look like he was wearing his resting bitch face, the stern expression that he put on when dealing with antagonistic opposing counsel. "All Dutch citizens carry a diplomatic passport. There are only fifty of us."

Rox said, "I call bullshit."

"Fine, but let's talk about this later."

"Oh, we will. You can count on that."

A small smile sneaked through his blank expression. "I suppose we shall."

Four more police cars sped into the parking lot, sirens blaring and rollers flashing. They surrounded the first police car and their SUV.

"Cash, is there something you need to tell me?" Rox raised her hands slowly, making no sudden moves that might be misinterpreted.

The police officers in the other cars hopped out, drew their handguns, and faced outward, surveying the parking lot around them.

"What the heck is going on?" Rox asked him.

"We've been the victim of a violent crime," Casimir said. "Surely the police are here to protect us."

The first police officer came back to the car and handed them back their identification. "Thank you, sir, ma'am. You're free to go. Do you require any additional assistance, a tow truck or medical assistance? Do you need a ride home?"

"Uh, no thanks?" Rox had never heard of a police officer offering someone a ride in California.

Back home, sure. Back home, a police officer might offer to drive you home if you were coming out of a bar and hadn't gotten into your car yet, just to make sure everyone got home safely.

But in California? That was weird.

"Thank you, officer," Casimir said. "We would appreciate a ride back to my house."

"We don't need a ride," Rox told him. "We could just call a cab, or I could call Brandy or Wren or somebody to give us a lift." She turned to the police officer. "I'm sure that we don't need to trouble you."

"I believe that you would be safer in an official vehicle with a police escort, ma'am," she said.

One of the other officers, also a woman, looked back over her shoulder and said, "You should accept our offer, sir. I'll drive you."

"I was the responding officer," the first police officer called back at her. When she turned her head, Rox could see that her black hair was braided into a complicated bun on the back of her head. "I'll drive them home."

"I took the diplomatic defensive driving course, and I outrank you," the other lady officer retorted.

"But I am the responding officer!"

Rox leaned over to Cash and whispered, "Lord Almighty, you haven't slept with both of them, have you?"

"No," Casimir said. "It's the diplomatic passport. It brings out the best in everyone."

She squinted at him, but she couldn't tell if he was kidding or not.

Casimir called out, "Thank you, officers. We would be most grateful for a ride home."

Chapter Sixty-Eight

THE HACIENDA, AGAIN

HARD WORK

CASIMIR

BLAIR BABYLON

The entourage of police vehicles dropped them off at Casimir's house.

Rox walked inside without holding on to anything. Waves of weakness ran up her legs. She was almost falling off her heels, and she stood inside the house right next to the door from the garage, leaning against the wall.

Casimir stood beside her and hung out of the doorway, waving at the retreating battalion of police cars. The garage door rattled down.

Rox had tried to slow her breathing down, but she was still panting, scared to her core. She wasn't going to let herself act like a scared little skunk. No way, no how.

Her hands tingled, though, and she couldn't seem to take a deep enough breath to calm the flutters in her chest.

Outside, the garage door thunked closed.

Casimir slammed closed the door beside her. He

grabbed her into his arms and pressed her against the wall, his mouth finding hers. He kissed her hard, pressing his mouth to hers and groping her waist and her ass.

She almost thought, *Wow, what's gotten into him?* but her body answered his, a hot blast of desperate emotion dragged raw by the spraying glass and bullets singing with death. Rox grabbed him with one arm around his neck, her other hand clutching his waist, and one leg wrapped around his thigh.

He groaned into her mouth and ground his hips against her. His lips opened on hers, and she angled her head to kiss him more deeply. He shoved at her suit jacket, tangling her arms in it as he tried to take it off of her. She yanked at the jacket to get it off, but he was already sliding his hand up her thigh to hike her skirt up around her waist and tugging at her underwear, sliding his fingers over her hip and downward.

His cool fingers slipped over the heated skin between her legs. Flutters trickled over her body, and Rox whimpered. His lips opened farther, and his tongue ran over hers, licking her tongue while his fingers slipped in the same rhythm over her clit.

She curled against him, craving every second of contact between his hand on her ribs and waist and the other one between her legs and needing to believe that he was alive, that she was alive, and that her world hadn't ended with a sniper's bullet or the explosion of a car crash.

He tore his mouth away from hers and dove for

her neck, lifting her from under her thighs and crushing her between his hard body and the wall. Rox cinched her legs around his back, pushing her slim skirt up farther around her waist.

One of her high-heeled shoes fell off behind his back, clattering on the Spanish tile floor.

He held her waist with one arm and fumbled with his pants with the other, and Rox tried to help by moving her leg but she kissed his jaw and his face, holding him around his shoulders, and breathed in the faint vanilla and spice of his cologne. His suit jacket and the collar of his white shirt kept getting in the way of where she wanted to lick and bite his neck, so she grabbed the knot of his tie and pulled, loosening it. His afternoon stubble felt like rough sand under her lips. When she nipped the tender skin over the pulse in his neck, his body jerked in her arms and between her legs.

Her legs were locked around his waist, and there was no way she could take her panties off now. He dragged the thin silk out of the way, and she felt him pushing at her core.

She threw her head back and moaned, knocking her head against the wall as her body took his cock inside. He growled against her neck, holding her up with his burly arms and pushing himself inside her. She slid down over him, taking him all inside. His hard erection filled her.

Casimir pumped hard into her, growling and biting her neck and shoulder where he had pulled her blouse aside. Rox squeezed her eyes shut, panting and calling his name, *"Casimir,"* over and over while he thrust into her.

"Rox." His hoarse voice grated like he was forcing air out of his throat as hard as he forced himself into her body. "Rox, I love you. Rox, come with me. Rox, come *now.*"

She ran her mouth over his neck again and up to his face. As her lips found the little bit of scarred skin on his cheek, his head twitched back, but she grabbed him around his neck and forced him back so she could kiss that scar, too. "Casimir, I love you. Casimir, all of you. Take me. Take me *hard.*"

He did, pinning her against the wall and grinding up into her. His lips were drawn back, baring his teeth, as he shoved himself inside of her. *"Come now."*

Every hard thrust of him rubbed her clit and that soft, sensitive streak inside, each shove filling her and spiraling her harder and tighter as she clung to him, crying out his name.

She was clawing at him, claiming him, clinging to him as he grunted, his cock deep inside of her. His polished shoes slipped on the Spanish tile as he shouted, jabbing into her as his muscular body spasmed.

The violence of the orgasm slammed into Rox, blinding her and forcing a scream from her lungs as she clung to him. Waves pounded through her body, and a deafening silence blasted into her.

When she could breathe, when she could see, Casimir was holding her in his arms, stroking her hair. Her mouth was open and slack as she gasped for air. He murmured, "I've got you. I've got you."

She whispered, "I know."

Casimir carried her to the couch, cradling her in his arms, and told her, "I almost lost you today." His arms tightened around her sides, and he whispered, "I want to marry you, *now*, tonight, but we can't. But I want to. I am desperate to."

Rox sat up and shoved him backward. "Are you serious?"

He looked straight at her with those emerald-green eyes of his, not laughing, not joking. "I asked Arthur to fly us to Las Vegas last night."

"What, the plane didn't have enough gas in it?"

He smiled a little on the left side of his mouth. "So you would have said yes?"

Her head swirled, shocked and yet it was so right. She didn't want to just date him like all the other women had. She couldn't have survived if he had ghosted on her.

"I, well, I don't know." She let herself smile back at him, just a little. "You didn't even ask me to marry you. That would have been pretty presumptuous, just ending up in Vegas and expecting me to marry you without even asking."

"You know that I'm arrogant as all Hell. I think that's how you have put it, dozens of times, maybe hundreds of times."

"You bet your butt, I have."

He gathered her back into his arms. "You know me too well."

"Yeah, I do." She wrapped her arms around him and held on. "And I still haven't said yes, yet."

"Duly noted." He sighed, his muscled body deflating in her arms. "There are some legal hoops to jump through first, anyway."

Rox could only think of one legal impediment to marriage. "Are *you* married to somebody else? I didn't think to ask *that.*"

Casimir chuckled. "No, I'm not married and never have been. I'll explain in a minute. I want to make sure we're properly locked in here. Stay away from the windows."

A wall of windows and French doors looked out over the ocean and sky. "I'm not sure that's even possible."

"I'll be right back."

Rox dragged her skirt down and curled up on the living room couch, watching the churning Pacific ocean for any sign of a submarine or a helicopter coming to attack them. She gathered all three cats into a pile on her lap while Casimir paced the hallways and rooms, rattling every window and door to make sure it was locked.

The cats were unsure why Rox was insisting that they all sit on her. Speedbump kept weakly lunging with his bum leg to get away and follow Casimir around the house. Rox had owned cats all of her life and knew just how to grab at the scruff of his neck to keep him on her lap. Speedbump kept jumping just a little just to see if he could get away, but he stayed.

Pirate sighed and swished his fluffy tail, gazing up at her with his single eye, but he seemed resigned to the fact that he was going to be sitting on her lap for a few minutes. She scratched the back of his neck, digging her fingers deeply into his thick fur, and he went limp.

Cash paced through the living room again, opening the door to the garage to check that the garage doors were down and locked, and then setting off for the guest room wing to check those doors and windows.

On his fourth time through, before he could leave again, Rox said, "Casimir, honey, why don't you sit down here with me for a minute?"

When he glanced at her, he must have realized the futility of checking the doors and windows for a fifth time, so he flopped beside her on the couch and wrapped his arm around her shoulders. The cats wandered away to lie around them. "I almost got you killed today."

"No, you didn't. Don't be silly, Cash."

"Casimir," he said.

"Okay, *Casimir* didn't almost get me killed, either. Some sniper almost killed both of us, but this wasn't your fault."

"I should have had security here."

"Look, you've obviously got quite a bit of money, but most people don't have hot and cold running security guards. Other than Maxence, evidently."

"Maxence and I have a lot in common. Right now, I need to call in professional security services."

"Wow. Mr. Fancy Pants can call in professional security services with just a phone call."

He looked down at her from the sides of his eyes without turning his head. "When I get done with this, we need to talk."

"Seriously? That offended you?"

"I'm not offended in the slightest, but we should talk." He pulled his phone out of his pocket and told it, "Call Ana."

Rox wanted to tease him that he was calling his sister like he would call his mommy, but he was on the phone. She could do it later.

And maybe Ana was actually a lady mercenary. You never knew.

Casimir spoke Dutch to his sister on the phone, so Rox couldn't even properly eavesdrop. He kept glancing at her though, and she was pretty sure that she heard her own name a few times. The Dutch language sounded kind of like German but with more *who's* and *hee-oo's* in it.

She definitely heard Ana squeal at least once.

He tapped the screen to hang up the call. "All right, we'll have security forces arriving tomorrow afternoon. We're to stay put and away from the windows."

"Is your sister in the army or something?"

"No. Well, technically I suppose she is, but nevertheless, she is sending people to retrieve us.

They will evacuate us to Amsterdam tomorrow. Do you have your passport with you?"

"Yeah, in my purse." She and Casimir had flown to meet clients overseas with an hour's notice more than once.

"Good."

"What about the cats?" she asked, stroking Pirate's scarred head.

"I'll ask my housekeepers to take care of them. They're very dependable. We should be gone for about a week. By the time we get back, we will have submitted the charges and evidence to the ethics committee, so all this will have blown over. It will be too late to stop the charges, so surely whoever hired the sniper won't pursue us after that."

"Are you sure?" she asked.

"Either way, we will have a significant security presence when we come back. No one will be able to touch us."

"So men with guns will protect us from the other men with guns?"

"They can be surprisingly effective." He paused and took both her hands in his. "I've done this all wrong."

"I told you that the sniper wasn't your fault. How could a *sniper* be anyone's fault?" she asked him.

"Not that." He slid off the couch and stood on one knee before her, still holding both her hands in his. Behind him, outside the French doors, the ocean frothed gray. "I've done this all wrong. Let me do it right. Roxanne Dolly Neil—"

Good Lord, he had remembered her middle name from that time they had gotten so drunk in Québec that she had admitted it to him.

"I have dreamed of this moment. I have loved you for years, and I finally have a chance to hold you, to show you how I feel, and I want to marry you."

He had carried her to her hotel room that night, and she thought that she had dreamed that he had kissed her on the forehead before he had gone through the adjoining door to his own room, but now she suspected that she hadn't been dreaming.

"*Lieveke,* will you do me the honor and privilege and become my wife, my princess, and I will love you and stay with you all the days of our lives?"

Rox drew in a breath to say yes. Her body was still trembling from him taking her against the wall. Her hands were shaking in his.

Everything that he said calmed her fears and let her heart beat again.

Movement.

She looked over his shoulder at the French doors and the ocean outside.

Outside the windows, something flashed in the sunlight.

Past the glass of the windows, something dropped like a bird crash-landing on the deck.

She pointed over his shoulder. "Casimir, what's—"

He twisted to look back where she was pointing and saw the little bundle lying on the deck.

He leapt across the couch at her.

She gasped, “What—”

His shoulders shoved her chest, flattening her on the couch. His arms closed around her head, and he crouched over her.

Fire blasted through the doors and into the room.

Chapter Sixty-Nine

CHOICE

HARD WORK
CASIMIR
2
BLAIR BABYLON

Scalding pain rushed over Casimir's back.

The fire flash was gone in an instant, but smoke was already rising in the house, and it stung his nose.

Screams burst all around him, driving into his ears. Shrieks blasted through the air as the fire alarm raged.

"Run." He pulled Rox to her feet. *"Run!"*

She stumbled, stunned by the blast. One of her shoes was gone, but she was moving toward the door to the garage.

Water showered down on him as the sprinklers sprayed, but the fire on the wall grew, crawling across the ceiling.

Casimir took a step. Something was under his foot. When he looked down, matted fur lay beside his shoe.

He grabbed the cat—Speedbump from the look of his sorry gray fur—and slung him over one arm.

The cat struggled weakly but didn't claw. Another step, and he found Midnight, the black cat, crouching behind the arm of the couch, pressing his face against the upholstery and trying to hide from the blaring alarm and shooting water. He grabbed Midnight by the scruff of his neck and tucked him next to Speedbump in his arm.

"Go!" he roared at Rox. *"Run!* Get the garage door open."

Rox ran for the door, hesitating to scoop up her purse and his briefcase from the floor on the way out.

Casimir still held the two cats, Speedbump and Midnight, under one arm.

Just two.

Pirate. The last cat, the hideous cat with one eye and chewed-down ears, had to be around here somewhere.

The curtains around the windows had caught fire, blazing and boiling smoke across the ceiling. The smoke was burning his eyes, and he scrubbed them with the back of his free hand.

A cat streaked across the floor, running for broken windows and the fire.

Casimir sprinted after him, reaching for his neck but missing. The other two cats clung to his arm, claws deep in his flesh, but they didn't struggle to get away.

Pirate, however, scrambled in a panicked run toward the fiery wall.

He sprinted after the cat.

The heat from the burning wall washed over him, singeing his eyebrows and eyelashes and scraping the skin on his face.

Casimir ran, chasing the fleeing animal. He crouched, grabbing at air. Finally, his hand found the fur behind the cat's neck, and he held on despite the cat's thrashing and clawing to get away.

Sparks popped from the wall near him, landing on his cheek above the scar from the car accident. He held the two other cats with that arm. He couldn't brush the sparks off.

The sparks burned his cheek over the cheek-bone, grinding into his flesh, and he couldn't do a damn thing about it without dropping at least one of them and abandoning them to the fire.

He couldn't drop them. Beyond the fact that they were living, feeling beings and he could not leave them in the burning house, Rox loved these hideous beasts, even though no one should love anything so monstrous.

Something dropped on his back, burning.

Casimir clutched all three cats and ran for the door to the garage, their tails and hind legs swinging against his stomach.

Chapter Seventy

DRIVING

Rox held the door to the passenger side of the car open, praying harder than she ever had in her life. *Please, God. Please let him make it out. What the hell was he doing?*

Heat from the fire was filling the garage, washing over her bare legs and feet. Even the cement floor was getting hotter. She didn't know how long she could wait before she ran out of the burning house and into the afternoon sunshine beyond the open garage door.

The door from the house flapped open. A spume of black smoke geysered out of the doorway like a dragon had spewed it. Casimir pushed his way out of the smoke, all three of her cats hanging from his arms. The smoke rolled across the ceiling and out of the open garage door.

"Get in! Get in the car!" she yelled.

Casimir stumbled down the steps from the house, bouncing off the wooden railing on the side with his hip. His body contracted and spasmed, and he coughed the smoke out of his lungs. Tendrils of smoke clung to him as he staggered across the garage. One of the cats was wheezing, too.

"Cash!" she yelled, waving toward the open car door.

He made it to the car without dropping any of the cats and toppled inside. Rox slammed the door closed behind him and ran around to the driver's side of the car. She jumped in, slammed her door, and floored the accelerator.

The tiny sports car raced out of the garage and down the long driveway toward the hills.

"Why did you stop?" she asked, shaking and failing to keep the hysteria out of her voice. "Why weren't you *right behind me?*"

"The cats ran the wrong way," he said, leaning back in the seat and brushing at his face. "I had to find Pirate."

"You shouldn't have followed them," she said. "You should have *run.*"

He closed his eyes. "But they most certainly would have died."

"You should have saved yourself."

"I couldn't just leave those hideous beasts," he said.

She gripped the steering wheel more tightly and pointed the car down the winding road. "You shouldn't have gone back. You should have *run.*"

"Just keep driving," Casimir said, carefully lifting the cats into the back of the car. The cats trickled off the seat and huddled together in the footwell behind his seat, a miserable clump of soggy fur. "Hopefully, no one stuck around to make sure that we died in there. We obviously weren't meant to survive that."

"But we did," she said. "We survived."

In the back seat, the cats wheezed, coughing pathetically as if someone were wringing out their little lungs.

"But we weren't supposed to," Casimir said, "and they didn't think that we would. They probably didn't take the sprinklers into account."

"How can you know what they were thinking? Do you know who it was?"

Casimir cranked himself around in the seat and looked out the back window as Rox sped through the hills. "If they had thought we might get out, there would have been a sniper on the hill, too."

"That's terrible! That's awful! How could anyone even think of such a thing?"

She glanced in the rearview mirror. A column of black smoke seethed into the sky.

Casimir dug through his briefcase that was lying on the seat in back. "We need to get out of here. We can't wait for Ana to send the reinforcements tomorrow afternoon. I'm calling Arthur and Maxence."

"But what good will that—" *Oh.* Arthur had a plane. Maxence had a personal military.

"I'm not sure how fast they can turn the plane around, but I'm hoping they can be here sooner than Ana's forces. Arthur!" he said into the phone, his voice suddenly jovial. "We've had a spot of trouble here, and we need a lift. Could you send that plane around for us?"

A speeding fire engine whizzed past them on the other side of the road, sirens blaring.

"Smashing," Casimir said. "And when would it be here?"

Rox drove silently, maneuvering the car down the winding road.

Casimir said, "First thing in the morning. *Excellent.* We'll just survive the snipers and firebombings on our own until then. Of course, I'm joking! But I'll tell you all about it on the plane tomorrow." He paused. "Slightly singed." Paused again. "If Maxence can do without them for a few hours, I would indeed appreciate his security." He hung up the phone. "We just have to survive the night."

"We'll just get a hotel," Rox said. "We'll find a hotel that will take animals or smuggle the motley crew in."

One of the cats howled, as if on cue.

Maybe the hotel would have a dryer. Her soggy clothes clung to her and smelled like meth-lab smoke.

"They will be looking for us," Casimir said. "Registering at a hotel might not be our safest option. Evidently, by giving Val an ultimatum, I seem to have tipped our hand. They want to prevent us from exposing Val and Josie to the ethics committee."

"Those bastards," Rox said, anger winding up in her chest. "Those bastards, that they would try to kill us like that. First a sniper, then a bomb. Those *assholes.*"

"Indeed," Casimir said, looking out the passenger-side window into the afternoon sun glancing off the hills.

Anger grabbed Rox, flushing through her body. She could feel her pounding heartbeat in her fists squeezing the steering wheel. "Those assholes think that they can burn your house down? They want to see things on fire? We'll show them fucking things on fire!"

Casimir glanced over at her.

"We'll show them so much fucking fire that they'll regret ever fucking with us," she said, her words grating in her throat and clenched teeth. "We'll show those assholes what it's like when *we* burn it *all* down."

"I don't think we should firebomb anyone," Casimir said. "We should just go to the ethics committee and let the repercussions take their natural course. They'll be disbarred. The clients will sue them and win. They are about to lose everything."

"Oh, no," she said. "They ran you off the road and nearly killed you, and then they shot at both of us, and then they threw a damn bomb and burned down your *house.* They want to see playing dirty?" She looked at him, her heart punching at her temples and wrists with rage. "They should not have messed with a Southern girl. I will fight fire with bright, cleansing fire. I will call down the wrath of God on them such as they have never seen. I will utterly destroy them, salt the Earth, and drive them into the sea."

Casimir had been watching her, a smile growing on his face. A livid burn crossed the scar on his left cheek. "God, you're beautiful when you're angry."

"You can call me beautiful some other time, Casimir. Right now, I am the vengeful angel of death and they shall rue the day they messed with me or the man I love."

"I love it when you're so angry that you become biblical."

Her brain spun. "We won't attack until the middle of the night. Until then, we need a place to hide."

"For a few hours," Casimir said.

"Phone Chick," Rox called into the air. She knew of one place where those bastards wouldn't dare look for her and Casimir.

"Yes, Your Imperial Majesty?" her car answered.

"That's what your phone calls you?" Casimir asked, laughing.

"My phone knows my personality better than anyone else," she said. "Call Brandy."

Brandy's battalion of enormous pit bulls would tear their damn legs off and eat them.

It would serve them right, too.

Chapter Seventy-One

BIG DOGS AND BRANDIWINE

HARD WORK

CASIMIR

BLAIR BABYLON

Rox and Cash stood on the sidewalk outside of the gate to Brandy's house.

Five slavering pit bulls leapt and frothed at the chain-link fence, just feet from where they stood. Most members of the pit bull breed are generally medium-sized dogs, but these creatures had obviously been bred from some mutant offshoot of the breed that had crossed pit bulls with buffalo.

Cash watched the dogs slam their boulder-like bodies against the steel mesh of the fence. "Are you sure it's safe to take the cats into the house?"

"Brandy will put the dogs up. They can stay locked up for a couple hours, probably." Assuming that they didn't chew their way through the steel bars of whatever cage Brandy put them in.

The door to the house opened. Brandy danced out, flitting on her tiptoes. The dogs parted for her, herding around her and respectfully wagging their tails. Not one of them jumped up on her.

"Rox! Are you okay?" Brandy held out her skinny arms as she walked.

Rox said, "Are you sure that you don't mind if we and the cats stay here for a few hours?"

"Not at all! I'll just corral the hellhounds." She led the dogs away to the back of the house and returned alone a minute later. She told Cash, "They're just overgrown puppies."

Cash smiled and nodded, ever the diplomat.

Brandy hugged Rox as she walked into the yard. "So you've had a rough day, haven't you?"

"I could really use a glass of sweet tea."

Brandy pet her hair and glanced back at Cash. "We'll have to find you something to wear. You're soaking wet."

"If I could just borrow a towel or something, these clothes should dry."

"Oh, I can probably find something you could wear."

He glanced down Brandy's diminutive body to her tiny shoes and raised an eyebrow. "All right."

Rox knew what they were getting into, but she didn't say anything. She wrapped her arm around Brandy's waist as they walked inside to hide out for a few hours until dark.

When they got into the living room, Rox paused and almost turned around to warn Casimir, but heck, he was a European, depraved sexual dominant who frequented BDSM clubs. Nothing should shock him, right?

An enormous four-poster bed, fifteen feet across, occupied most of the living room.

A probably naked white man was chained to one corner of the bed. A sheet covered his midsection. He grinned at them, and one of his hands flapped, waving, even though an iron manacle chained his wrist to the intricately carved bedpost.

Brandy's other two husbands were probably around somewhere, maybe tied up, maybe doing the dishes, probably naked.

Casimir stopped in the doorway, taking it all in.

His expression was his classic resting bitch face, not a flicker of emotion.

Rox couldn't wait to grill him on what he was thinking.

Instead, she asked Brandy, "Honey? After we bring in the cats, we need to work on some things before we go out tonight for our little errand. Could we steal some WiFi, please?"

BREAKING AND ENTERING

HARD WORK

CASIMIR

2

BLAIR BABYLON

"So, this is technically burglary," Rox said.

In the dark law office, they held their cell phones out in front of them, using the flashlight app to see. The beams swept through the black air, illuminating circles of the blue cubicles where the admins and paralegals worked and shining white glares on the walls and plants. Computer screens glinted in the beams.

Casimir shook his head. He looked just like a stereotypical burglar, wearing black sweatpants and a matching sweatshirt, which fit his trim waist rather better than they had Brandy's chubby but very tall husband. He said, "Burglary is breaking and entering with the intent to commit a felony while on the premises. We might be breaking and entering, or at least entering, but we do not intend to commit a felony. We only intend to send a few emails."

More like a few thousand.

Rox smiled and hoisted her heavy purse back up on her shoulder. "Yes. Yes, we will. And that's all."

They walked between the cubicles, watching the shadows created by their flashlight beams, until they got to Rox's office. A shiny brass knob had been installed on the door. "That's new."

"I figured that they would change the locks to our offices. I was shocked that my keycard worked in the main entrance."

Rox glanced around the office, looking for movement or red dots from a sniper's laser sight. "You don't think this is a trap, do you?"

"I think that they assume we're dead." Cash looked around the darkened office, scanning over the tops of the cubicle dividers. "At least, I hope that they think we're dead."

Rox bit her lip, staring at the doorknob. "They must have changed our office locks right after we left, but they didn't bother to change the front door code after the firebomb."

Casimir nodded. "So Val and Josie must have known about that."

"Dammit, I hate those guys." Rox jiggled the doorknob on her office door, but it didn't turn. "Shit."

Casimir said, "Stand back."

Rox stepped away, and Casimir leaned to his side and kicked the door hard. It popped open and slammed into the wall behind it, spraying wood from the doorjamb into the office.

"Did you take karate at some point?" Rox asked.

"Tae kwon do."

They walked into her office, and Rox shut the door behind them. It drifted open a little because the latch was very broken. "What else do I not know about you?"

Even in the low light, she saw him flinch. "We'll talk about that on the plane."

They ran around to the other side of the desk, rolling her big office chair back and away, and Rox tugged her computer out of her purse. Her big rubber plant was still there, and she felt bad about abandoning it.

She set her laptop on the desk and opened the lid. The token had fallen to the bottom of her purse, and it took her a minute to fish it out. The blue glow from the computer screen washed over the token, and Rox held it in both hands, angling the tiny stick toward the computer so that she could see the numbers on it.

Casimir lit the flashlight on his phone again and shone the light on her hands and the small security device.

They watched the token, waiting, until the nine digit number changed with a flash.

Rox scrambled to type her identification number into the computer and then type the security code displayed on the token in the next box.

She tapped the Enter key, and the law firm's home screen zoomed into view.

"I'll be damned," she said. "They didn't disable my security ID, either. Those bastards must've really thought that we were dead. I thought that I was going to have to use Wren's, but I didn't really want to get her into trouble."

Rox navigated to the folder with the master client list.

Casimir walked over to the window beside her door and peered through it, watching the dark office.

"See anything?" she asked.

"No." He kept watching at the window, anyway.

Rox downloaded the entire client list, hundreds of names and email addresses, onto her laptop. "I've got the emails. They didn't add any extra layers of security after they fired us."

"Good. Go ahead."

"Are you sure? I was pretty angry when we wrote this."

"We edited it, and the clients need to know. It sounds professional. I wouldn't let anything unprofessional go out, and I don't think you would either. If for any reason we don't make it to the plane, or if the file doesn't make it to the ethics committee, the clients need to know."

That thought chilled her. They—whomever they were—had nearly killed Casimir in that car accident, and they had made two more attempts on both of them within the last day.

Yeah, they needed to send the emails now.

Rox fired up the email management system and pasted in the letter that she and Casimir had written. Under the careful, polite language, the words seethed with rage on their clients' behalf. The clients, all those actors and singers and musicians and writers, had been bilked out of millions upon millions of dollars, and they damned well deserved to know it.

She imported the email list, doing it manually instead of using the list in the email server to make sure that she got absolutely every client that Arbeitman, Silverman, and Amsberg had ever had. She added her own email address at the bottom so that she could make sure that the email went out.

The email program ground, sending the emails.

Rox's phone pinged, indicating an email had arrived. She checked it, and it was indeed their message.

Which meant that thousands of other emails had gone out, too, and thousands of clients were going to start calling Val, Josie, and other lawyers as soon as they saw them. Some of those people were on the East Coast, which meant that they were probably already out of bed.

"Okay. I'm done." She slapped the lid of her laptop closed.

"So that's it. We burned it all down. Val and Josie will have nothing left after the clients go after them." Casimir shook his head. "It took Val decades to build this law firm, and it will be gone."

"It's chopping down a tree that is rotten to the core. She was screwing over our clients. They deserved her honesty. They deserved her best work for them."

Casimir sighed. "Yes, they deserved her honesty, and the others at the firm deserve ours."

"Come on. Let's go. Arthur's plane will be waiting for us."

"I can't leave," Casimir said.

Rox huffed up. "I beg your pardon!"

"The other admins and paralegals here—Wren, Melanie, and all the rest—they deserve our honesty. They deserve to know what we've done."

"Val and Josie tried to kill us! Several times!"

"They won't do it themselves. The rest of them deserve to know the truth." He sighed again. "I have to stay and tell them what we did and what's coming."

"You can't stand up there and tell them that you just burned down the law firm and got them all fired."

"I can tell them that Val and Josie have been cheating the clients, and they need to look for other employment. Full disclosure is the most ethical path, here. Also, I'll be passing out my phone number in case they need a reference."

Rox rolled her eyes at him. "They're not going to like it. They-all might try to tear you limb from limb."

He shrugged. "I doubt it will come to that, but you should go to the plane."

Rox rolled her eyes harder at him. "I'm not leaving you here with those animals."

He pushed up his sleeves, baring the dark, fiery tattoos on his left arm and the tatt with the three shields just above the inside of his right wrist. "They should be here in a few hours."

PLEADING WITH THE ANGELS

HARD WORK
CASIMIR
BLAIR BABYLON

Rox and Casimir dozed in her wide office chair for a few hours. They had only slept a little before they had broken into the office in the wee hours of the morning, staying up to write the email and strategize.

Before that, one of Brandy's husbands had cooked a proper Italian meal that had taken five courses and four hours to eat. Rox had done her best to do justice to the homemade pasta and tender chicken piccata.

Brandy had leaned over to her, gesturing with a glass of red wine toward the solidly built man, who wore jeans and a red tee shirt with the name of some Italian soccer team printed on it. He and Casimir had immediately started talking international football. She said to Rox, "Now you know why I keep Antonio around."

Rox nodded and slurped a string of spaghetti into her mouth. The subtle herbs and savory meat sauce on it lingered on her tongue, and she hummed with happiness.

Dang, Rox would keep a guy who could cook like that chained to the stove, too.

Maybe not as literally as Brandy did.

She was still dreaming of the lemon sauce on the chicken piccata.

In the chair, dozing on Casimir's lap, Rox snuggled farther into his arms. He adjusted, wrapping her up more tightly, and he nuzzled her hair for a second before leaning his head back and going to sleep.

It still didn't feel real, holding him like this. Every now and then, a wisp of jealousy ran through her that other women from the office, *a lot of them,* might have lain in his arms like this, but she stopped herself.

First of all, Rox had been supposedly married and hadn't wanted to deal with The Randy Tomcat of Los Angeles.

Secondly, the relationships that he had had with other women had just been about the sex and the adventure, and only about the sex and the adventure. She held on tightly to the thought that they had been friends for years.

Thirdly, both Wren and Melanie had said that Casimir wasn't all lovey-dovey with them. He had been fun and other things, but not affectionate, and he never mentioned the future or pretended like they had had a real relationship.

Casimir sighed in his sleep, his muscular chest rising and falling under her hand.

Maybe *this* time, or maybe with *her,* maybe *he* would be different.

Maybe he wouldn't ghost on her.

Casimir had been down on one knee and proposed to her with her whole name right before the bomb had gone off.

Maybe he hadn't been screwing around.

His eyes hadn't looked like he was screwing around. His brilliant green eyes had looked seriously at her, maybe with just a touch of longing in his breathless voice.

She hadn't said yes to him yet, and she fully intended to string him along as long as she could. That heartbreaker was going to *suffer.*

Her whole body vibrated, hoping, pleading with the angels, that he wasn't kidding her.

She rested her head against his shoulder, his whole body wrapped around her, and closed her eyes.

SPEECH

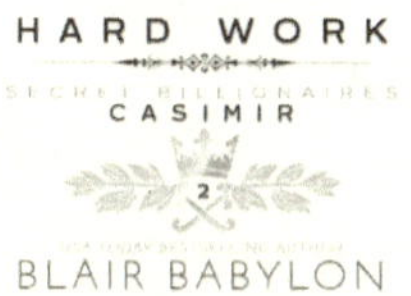

Rox and Casimir were standing inside her darkened office, leaning against the wall.

They had stood there, quietly talking, holding hands, out of the lines of sight of the people slowly filling the main floor. His hand wasn't tight around hers, but his fingers held hers firmly, like he was holding on.

She asked, "What are you going to say?"

"I'm not sure," he mused.

"Going to let the Blind Spirit of Justice move you?"

"Maybe. And hoping that certain ancestors were also demagogues, in addition to whatever else they did in life, and that it's genetic."

"Okay, then."

"What time is it?" he asked, even though he was holding his phone.

Rox consulted her own phone. "Nine-oh-seven."

"Is Wren out there?"

"Let me text." She paused, and her eyebrows rose. "Yeah, she's early today."

Casimir looked at his own phone. "All right, we've got five minutes. Let's go."

"Five minutes to what?" But Casimir had already opened the office door and was walking out into the main floor area.

Rox trotted after him. "Hey! Five minutes to what?"

When she yelled, people turned. A wave of silence propagated through the large center area of the law office. At the disruption, heads popped up over the short upholstered walls like prairie dogs emerging from their holes to look for predators.

Casimir's stride lengthened. At six-four, he was easily tall enough to see over the cubicle dividers, but he leapt up onto a desk in the center of the room. It swayed under his legs for a moment and he looked down at it, but he kept his balance.

Casimir announced, "May I have everyone's attention, please?"

Rox almost giggled. Sometimes that British accent of his was jarring.

He snapped his fingers in the air. "Everyone? For just a moment?"

Who snapped their fingers to get people's attention? Only a Brit. Or a guy who was Dutch but whom everyone thought was a Brit because he didn't tell anyone anything about himself that he didn't have to.

Rox clutched her purse more closely to her stomach, suddenly fearful for him.

Casimir said, "I need to talk to you all. The car accident that injured me a few months ago was a murder attempt. After I was fired yesterday, there were two more attempts to kill Rox and myself: a sniper shot at us as we drove home on the freeway—"

A collective gasp withdrew the air from the room, and the muttering amplified as the admins and paralegals remembered seeing the sniper shootings on the news the previous night and discussed it among themselves.

One woman asked, "They were shooting at you guys?"

He said, "We were in the SUV that was initially attacked. Rox was driving."

The field of faces, hundreds of them, all turned toward Rox, scrutinizing her and her total lack of make-up and too-tight gym clothes that she had borrowed from Brandy.

She waved, swiveling her hand like the Queen. She could feel that her face had scrunched up into an uncomfortable grin that looked more like she was baring her teeth at them. Damn, of all the times that she should have been ready with her resting bitch face plus prim smile.

"Rox was almost killed, too?" Wren shrieked.

Casimir said, "Both by the sniper and when they firebombed the house."

This time, the mutter swelled into chatter and talking.

Someone yelled, "A *bomb?*"

"Yes. Bombs were thrown at my house last night. It burned. The house was entirely destroyed."

Gasps.

More talking.

Grumbling.

Angry mutters.

"That was *your* house on the news last night?"

"Unfortunately," Casimir said.

"You should sue the hell out of them!"

Rox almost laughed, and she bowed her head to swing her hair forward around her face.

Wren called out to her, "Rox, are you okay?"

Rox nodded. "Yeah, I'm fine."

Casimir glanced at his phone. "We believe that the reason why these attempts on our lives have been occurring is that there have been some gross irregularities in the contracts that we have been approving for clients. I have found clauses in the contracts that Valerie Arbeitman and Josie Silverman worked on that are egregiously unethical. I have confirmed that these contracts were actually signed by all parties. I believe that Val and Josie were approving these contracts and allowing agents and studios to swindle our clients."

A mutter cascaded through the room. People looked at each other, squinting and frowning.

A woman's voice said, "But that's illegal."

Someone else yelled, "So is shooting people and burning down houses."

A nervous giggle rose from the crowd.

Casimir glanced at his phone again. He looked back up at all of their friends and coworkers. "Murder and swindling clients are both illegal. That's why I have informed all of our current and previous clients that they may have problematic clauses in their contracts and that they may have recourse in the civil and criminal courts. *All* of them."

This time, no one said anything.

Silence spread over the room as everyone realized that all of the law firm's clients were going to call the office that morning.

Every single one of them.

Except for a few who would go straight to their own lawyers.

"I'm sorry to leave you with this," Casimir continued, "but I suggest that you all look for new employment. If you need a reference, I will be happy to provide one. I believe that Val and Josie will be too busy with their own legal and civil defenses to write references." Casimir looked at his phone one more time and thumbed something on the screen. He held out his hand to Rox, and she moved closer to where he stood on the desk. Holding his phone near his mouth, he looked right in her eyes and said into the phone, "Go."

"What did you do?" Rox asked him.

"One minute." He looked out over the room,

surveying everyone assembled there. He spoke loudly and said, "I regret that this law firm is ending in this manner. Swindling our clients was a criminal and unethical act. I tried to handle the problem in-house. My plan had been to close down the office in stages so that we could find positions for everyone at other firms, but they fired me yesterday, and the problems are too extensive."

Another woman called out, "Are we going to be arrested?"

"I can't imagine that would be the case. Val and Josie seem to have inserted these clauses after the paralegals had signed off on them. It appeared to be their actions alone."

A sigh of relief lifted into the air above the assembled admins and paralegals.

A voice called out of the crowd, "Where will you be, Cash?"

Cash? Oh, yeah. *Cash.* Rox shook her head, trying to wrap her mind around all the names.

He said, "I'll be overseas for few days. I will email Wren and Melanie with my phone number, and they will disseminate it."

The glass doors at the front of the office slammed open.

Rox spun, her fists up and ready to commit mayhem on whomever was coming to attack her and Casimir. Time to fight fire with fire and salt the Earth.

Two columns of men in black fatigues marched in and drove a wedge through the crowd toward

Casimir and Rox. Bulky belts circled their waists, providing them with multiple deadly options. They didn't have their guns drawn, but they all wore snapped holsters on their hips.

So many of them. Better to run.

She shrank closer to Casimir's legs, ready to push him toward the fire exits.

Casimir hopped down from the table and stood beside her. He wrapped an arm around her shoulders. "The cavalry has arrived."

Rox recognized one of the dark-clad guys leading the twenty or so men as Hugo Faure, Maxence's head of security who had been in charge when they had flown to The Devilhouse, and she blew out a pent-up breath.

For a second there, that battalion of men had looked like the government's men in black had shown up to kidnap them for knowing too much about certain unidentified aircraft.

Hugo Faure stood next to Casimir, his back toward him, facing out at the crowd. "How bad is this situation?"

"Just a group of friends." Casimir shoved his phone into his pocket.

"I've seen friendlier people behind a rifle," Hugo said, watching the crowd.

"They've had some bad news," Casimir told him, his voice low, "and they're about to have a very bad day."

Rox stood close to him, and one of the men in black gave her a quick side-eye from behind his dark sunglasses and then continued to examine the law firm's staff around him.

Hugo touched his ear. "Let's go."

The security men condensed their formation around Rox and Casimir, and the phalanx moved as a single group toward the doors. The crowd of admins and paralegals parted as the security men stiff-armed them aside, and Rox hurried to keep up with the long-legged men.

She walked out the glass doors of the law office just as Hugo muttered to Casimir, "Mr. Grimaldi said that you had extensive security at your compound."

Casimir smirked. "Maxence might have been mistaken."

"Damn it. He does that all the time. It drives his uncle and myself mad."

Casimir laughed out loud at that.

Hugo grumbled, "So His Highness has not had proper security the whole time that he was in California."

Rox stopped in the hallway leading to the elevator and whirled around. "What did you call Maxence?"

Surely Hugo was being sarcastic.

Surely he was calling Maxence an entitled little prince-jerk because he was a spoiled rich kid.

Yeah, that made sense.

Of course, the security guy would disparage the man who had built a school with his own hands in an African war-ravaged village and was too skinny when he came back because he gave his food to little girls. There was lots of privileged, entitled attitude to mock there.

Yeah, that made no sense at all.

"Mr. Faure!" Rox called out because she was a proper little Southern girl. "What did you call Maxence?"

But Hugo had stepped back, one of his arms spread wide and the other resting on the butt of his gun, as the security men bustled her and Casimir into the elevator and out of the building, to where black SUVs idled at the curb, waiting.

Casimir held her elbow and led her toward the cars.

Another of the security men said to Casimir, "This way, Your Highness."

Rox stopped dead in her tracks.

One of the other security guys danced around her, his arms raised, rather than run her over.

Casimir stood, staring at her, his green eyes wary, looking to see if she had heard.

Oh, she had *heard* all right.

She braced her fists on her hips. "And what did he just call *you?*"

Chapter Seventy-Five

CODENAME: LUMBERJACK PRIME

HARD WORK

CASIMIR

2

BLAIR BABYLON

In the SUV, Rox and Casimir sat on the very ends of the seat, as far away from each other as they could get. She rolled the hem of Brandy's faded workout shirt between her fingers.

Casimir looked out the window of the SUV. The morning sun shone on the hard angles and planes of his face, glinting in the auburn scruff of his growing beard. He wouldn't even look at her, and he was wearing his impassive bitch face, repressing all emotion, as if they were in an enemy lawyer's office.

She said, "That guy wasn't serious. That guy was just joking around because suddenly you need all this security, right? That's why he called you 'Your Highness.'"

"Rox, we should discuss this in private." His reserved, cultured English accent sounded very foreign to her.

She cracked her knuckles, and her shoulders relaxed. Just because he was filthy rich didn't mean that he was actually royalty. "You're just screwing with me, right. Of course, you are. I'm the Queen of Sheba, too."

Casimir didn't reply. Even though the back seat of the SUV had a lot of legroom, his long legs still folded like a grasshopper behind the seat in front of him.

Rox looked at him, *really* looked at him. With his slim, elegant build, confident bearing, and the sweet and subtle scent of oodles and oodles of money, it kind of made sense that someone had called him Your Highness.

Her head boggled.

Just then, her phone buzzed in her purse, indicating an incoming text.

Probably someone from the office.

Probably *everyone* from the office.

She paused in her internal tirade.

Rox called her phone's voice prompt "Phone Chick."

And her phone called her "Your Imperial Majesty."

Like a code name.

These men were security guys, like the Secret Service.

One of these guys had called Casimir "Your Highness." Another one of the guys had called Maxence "His Highness," *exactly the same thing.*

Or, you know, *really close.*

Didn't the Secret Service give the President of

the United States a nickname like Bald Eagle One or Lumberjack Prime or something?

Of course. That must be it.

It was a security guy codename thing.

See? Easy answer.

Rox said, “So, ‘Your Highness’ is what these security guys call the person that they’re protecting, isn’t it? It’s just a code word or something. So that the bad guys won’t know who they’re talking about. Whoever the bad guys are. Because there are always bad guys.”

Casimir continued to stare out the window of the SUV, the morning sunlight glowing on his face, and didn’t agree with that obvious explanation.

Rox crossed her legs away from him and watched the city slip behind the SUV as they traveled.

The caravan stopped at Brandy’s house. Rox unlocked her door and began to open it.

Casimir touched her arm. “Don’t.”

She looked around the perfectly normal neighborhood. Short chain-link fences bounded the properties’ gravel front yards, and some of the houses could use a fresh coat of paint over the peeling bits, but it was fine. “What?”

“The security detail will get the cats,” he told her.

The neighborhood around Brandy’s house was a perfectly normal suburban neighborhood. It was a little on the old and cheap side when compared to the nicer part of Los Angeles, and some of the folks were sitting on their porches and peering at the caravan of tinted-window black SUVs, probably because their air-conditioning was broken again. It wasn't a gang neighborhood. Rox always felt perfectly safe coming here, except for Brandy's hellhound-variety pit bulls. No one felt safe around those rabid monsters except Brandy.

"What?" she asked. "I'll grab my cats. It's fine."

"This is how things are done. When we're in Amsterdam, you'll need to get used to it."

"We can't take the cats to Amsterdam," she exclaimed.

Casimir flipped his hand in the air, brushing off her concerns. "My nieces and nephews will love them."

Rox grabbed her purse. "Don't you need, like, a veterinary passport and a whole bunch of paperwork to take cats on an airplane and travel internationally?"

"Sometimes. Not this time." Casimir just continued to look at the window, watching.

More tremors started in Rox's stomach. "Why not?"

Casimir continued to stare out the window. "We'll talk about it later, in private."

Chapter Seventy-Six

THE HUGGER

HARD WORK

CASIMIR

BLAIR BABYLON

The cats hid under the seats of the SUV and yowled all the way to the airport, which was a mercifully short trip.

The last time Rox had flown through the private terminal, just a day and a little bit before, she had been so flustered at the idea of flying on a private jet and had been peering out the enormous wall of glass on the back side of the terminal at all the private planes coming and going that she hadn't really looked around the building.

On the way back, she had been too shell-shocked to look around.

The terminal was nice.

Have you ever seen a movie that takes place in the 1800s, maybe in Africa, where the whole point of the ostentatious, sumptuous, disgusting setting is obviously social commentary to emphasize that the imperial empire in the movie is so decadent, so morally failing, that they must be raping the land and enslaving the people to make it look like that?

Yeah. *That.*

In the movie, shining and soft leather upholsters every chair and couch. Cut crystal glasses and stemware sparkle in the tropical sun, which must have been packed in straw and tissue and imported from somewhere far away at great expense. The waiters, who are bowing obsequiously while they bring people drinks that cost a hundred dollars a glass, are all beautiful specimens of humanity, as decorative as the real art on the walls, and huge vases of riotous flowers bloom on every table, and the thick rugs cushion your feet.

Yep.

Rox didn't move her head, just her eyeballs, as she scanned the luxury that the rich people indulged in before they went out to their private jets.

She was torn between wanting it all for herself and wanting to burn it all down. People were starving. Dang, that champagne that the waiter offered her from a tray was delicious.

Hugo said, "This way, please."

Casimir held her elbow and steered her through the airport terminal as if Rox didn't know where to go.

The slim jet waiting outside the windows shone silver in the sunlight except for its tail, which was a grayed federal blue and emblazoned with three gold crowns. She hadn't noticed the paint job the other night.

She didn't even need to look at Casimir's tattoo on his right forearm to see if the tail fin matched one of the three shields. It totally did.

They crossed the tarmac, Casimir's hand still guiding her elbow, and climbed the stairway to the plane.

Inside, two security guys saw them and stood back, relaxing.

Maxence was sitting in one of the white leather recliners, his hands on his knees, eyes closed.

Arthur was standing in the aisle, bracing himself on two chairs, his back to them.

When they ducked to come in the doorway, Arthur's head whipped around, and he strode down the aisle and grabbed them both around their necks in a headlock, dragging Casimir against his shoulder and short little Rox against his side.

Her face was smashed against Arthur's dark blue suit and his ribs underneath.

She tried to push away, pressing her hand against his side, but Arthur's elbow was cinched around her neck. Even though the fine fabric of his suit and shirt separated her palm from his body, muscles bulged under her hand. Yep, Arthur was ripped under there.

She pushed away a little harder because he was really hanging onto her.

Arthur whispered, his voice hoarse, *"What the hell is going on with you two?"*

From the other side of Arthur, Casimir said, his voice slightly strangled, "Rox, I forgot to mention that Arthur cannot keep it British when he's upset. He becomes a *hugger.*"

Arthur shook them both, rattling them with his arms around their necks. "You two will stay in Amsterdam or London. You aren't coming back to this hellhole. If you need security, Caz, I will supply it. *Do you understand me?*"

Casimir pounded Arthur on the back. "I assure you, once we get home to Amsterdam, my sister won't let me take a piss without a team securing the facilities."

Beyond Arthur's arm, back in the seats, Maxence had opened his eyes and was staring at them. He blew out a very deliberate breath and slumped in his chair.

"You scared me shitless, you assholes." Arthur jiggled them some more, as if ensuring they were real. "A sniper and firebombs in *one damn day.*"

Rox gave up and wrapped her arms around Arthur's waist, hugging him back.

His arm loosened around her neck, and his hand relaxed down to the middle of her back. "I saw the footage. It looked like a coordinated terrorist attack. That's what they're calling it, you know. They're denying that it was aimed at one person and are bringing in federal authorities."

"But we're fine," Casimir told him, pounding him on the back. "We're fine, and we're here now."

Arthur released them, almost throwing himself backward, and straightened his shirt cuffs under his suit jacket.

Rox stumbled but grabbed a seatback to steady herself.

"Jackasses," Arthur muttered.

Casimir reached over the seats, extending his hand to Maxence, who stood and calmly shook his hand.

Maxence said, his voice low and cultured, "I'm very pleased to see you."

"And you. Thank you for the use of your men."

Maxence waved it off. "I was gratified to hear that they had secured you and that you were en route to the plane."

Arthur edged past them and walked up to the front of the airplane, leaning into the cockpit. He told the pilot, "Get us out of here."

The engines whined, winding up.

Rox found a seat and stowed her purse that held, as far as she knew, everything that remained of all her possessions in the world. Her other possessions were supposed to be in storage, moved there by the property company that owned her apartment building, but she hadn't been able to take that key and look, yet. Everything that she had taken with her had probably burned up or been soaked in the fire at Casimir's house.

Three more security men climbed the ramp, each holding one of her cats. They held the beasts securely, one arm around their bellies and the other hand grabbing the scruffs of their necks. The cats looked terrified and simultaneously insulted at the indignity. Pirate was on the verge of snarling.

A flight attendant swung the door closed with a *thunk* and spun the ship's wheel to secure it.

The three security men lowered the cats to the floor, releasing them.

All three cats swarmed Rox, piling onto her lap and shoulders and purring hard.

Chapter Seventy-Seven

VAN ORANJE-NASSAU VAN AMSBERG

Càsimir lowered himself into the seat beside Rox, stretching his legs under the table and under the chair across from him until his ankles touched the bottom of it.

Not enough leg room, as always.

No wonder Maxence and Arthur had claimed the couch in back with the television where they could stretch out.

He commandeered Pirate from Rox, dragging the huge ginger cat onto his own lap and petting the beast's broken ears. The stumps felt crispy along the edges, and Casimir was careful to be very gentle as he sank his fingers into the cat's deep fur.

Well, this had to be done. "Can we talk after we change planes in London? We'll be alone at that point, or at least Arthur and Maxence won't be around."

"No," Rox said, her sweet brown eyes stretched

wide with anger. "We need to talk now. I feel like I don't even know you."

"You know me," he said quietly. "You know me better than anyone else in the world. I've never lied to you."

She rolled her big, brown eyes and scoffed, "You need to talk to Maxence about sins of omission."

He nodded and stroked Pirate, who was crouching on his lap. He had known exactly what he had omitted all these years. Time to make reparations. "Ask me anything."

Rox had a beautiful, heart-shaped face, even when her little jaw was grinding her teeth in anger. She asked, "What's your real name?"

"Casimir Friso van Amsberg."

"Really?"

He bit his lip. "My baptismal name is Casimir Friso David Constantijn Christof, and my surnames are theoretically van Oranje-Nassau van Amsberg, but that almost never comes up."

"David?"

"As is traditional, I'm named after my four godfathers."

"Holy cow. That sounds like Dumbledore. He had 'Brian' in the middle of a whole bunch of weird names."

He nodded, staring at the cat in his lap. Rox had pressed him to read the Harry Potter books years ago, and he had read all seven of them. He liked her fun, fanciful taste in books. "I suppose it's incongruous."

"What country are you really from? Are you British?"

He glanced at her, watching to see if she thought that. "I am Dutch. I haven't ever lied to you."

"And yet you have a longer name than anyone I've ever met, and I didn't know half of it."

He bit his lip. "Van Amsberg is the name of my great-grandfather, who was German. I told you about him."

Rox waited, stroking the cats in her lap. Speedbump buried his face under her arm.

He finished, "And Oranje-Nassau is the name of my House."

"House," she said.

"Like the House of Windsor or Romanov or Hannover."

"So you're not House Hufflepuff."

A smile lifted one side of his mouth. "Nothing wrong with Hufflepuff. They're loyal. There's a lot to be said for loyalty."

"I would have totally pegged you for a Ravenclaw."

They'd had this discussion dozens of times, and it always came out the same way. "But Ravenclaws are evil."

"No. They're just smart. And kind of evil. And you're a lawyer. So yeah, you're definitely a Ravenclaw." She looked down at the cats. "Are Arthur and Maxence some sort of royalty, too?"

"Arthur is not a member of a royal family, and

we never allow him to forget it. Maxence plans to renounce everything for the Church."

Casimir heard a man's cough behind them that sounded like "asshole." When he glanced back, Arthur was laughing at them, as always.

Rox was still staring at him, watching him. "And yet Arthur's plane has three crowns on the tail fin."

"Not crowns. Coronets."

"Oh, and I suppose that there's a difference."

"There's a difference."

She grabbed Casimir's right arm and pushed up his sleeve, baring his forearm with the three-shield tattoo. Her hand warmed his wrist. "Three coronets, then. Just like your tatt."

The plane jerked and rolled backward, pulling away from the terminal.

He turned his arm over so that the morning sunlight streaming in the porthole window shone on the ink on his skin. "The blue shield with the three coronets is Arthur. The red and white harlequin pattern stands for Maxence. The Dutch lion on an orange field is mine."

"For the Orange Nassau house."

"For Hufflepuff."

"Oh, stop." She backhanded him on the shoulder, just like always. For years, he had prodded her so that she would slap his shoulder and grin. He loved every time she did it.

He explained, "We got them just before we left school. It's a pledge of mutual support. The centerpiece between the three shields," a triangle filled with what looked like a tangled rope, "is a Celtic knot that symbolizes friendship."

"And that's how your sister knew to call them." She inspected the tattoo more closely. "It looks kind of faded."

The ink under his skin had blued somewhat in over a decade. "It was done twelve years ago. We were seventeen."

The plane coasted to a stop and reversed, rolling forward. Outside the round window of the airplane, domed hangars and industrial buildings cast black shadows on each other in the morning sunlight.

"So the Dutch lion symbolizes the royal house." Rox bit her lip.

So tempting. This conversation must go well so that he would get the chance to bite it again, perhaps tonight.

She asked, "So what *should* I have been calling you, all these years?"

"Casimir."

"No. *Really.*"

"It's my name. It's what my mother and sisters call me. Arthur calls me 'Caz' because he can't be bothered with three syllables."

From several rows behind them, Arthur snorted.

"It doesn't matter what my last name is. It doesn't matter what family I was born into. I don't plan on ever going back to the Netherlands except for family functions. I will not live there." He hadn't quite meant to allow that sharp edge in his voice.

Her eyebrows rose. "You don't like the Netherlands?"

He scratched the gnarled scar and new burn on his cheek. In his head, he was insisting that it itched, but the blistered, charred skin still burned. "I prefer living elsewhere, quietly."

Rox turned toward him in her seat, upsetting Speedbump and Midnight, who grumbled before they settled down on her lap again. "Tell me why."

He scratched the new scars on his cheek again, a nervous move. "I told you about the car accident when I was six."

Rox took his hand, and he tightened his fingers around hers. Pirate nibbled on his arm when he stopped petting him.

"After the accident, some people were not kind, even though I was a child."

"A *small* child."

From behind them, Casimir heard Arthur sneeze, except it sounded like he said, "Willem," under his breath.

They didn't need to go into that, yet.

Casimir said, "One particular newspaper was abusive, following me around and taking pictures, jumping out at me because I looked particularly monstrous when surprised. The pictures ran with amusing captions."

Rox slid her hand up to his elbow and tucked her fingers around his thick biceps. He concentrated on Pirate in his lap and Rox's hand on his arm. He had learned as a child not to let his emotions show. A crying monster looks far worse than a stoic one.

"There's no reason for me to permanently reside in Amsterdam. An investigation will determine whether I should return to Los Angeles. I suspect not."

"Yeah, I don't think you can go back there," she agreed.

"I have the whole rest of the world."

Rox stroked his arm, fretting over him. "I'm sorry. That must have been awful."

Casimir shrugged. "It was a long time ago."

The new burn still felt like fire on his skin.

"If you want, I have some gauze and paper tape in my purse for," she gestured to her own cheek, "you know."

Anger boiled up in him, but he didn't let it show in anything more than an eyebrow twitch. "Let them look. Let them take pictures and talk."

"Good Lord, what did they say?"

Her horror at his response suggested that he hadn't been entirely successful in pressing that down. "That I should give up my spot in the line of succession in favor of my brother Willem, just in case anything happened to my sister, because no one wanted their prince or a king to look like a monster."

Rox's sweet eyes widened, this time with sympathy. "They said that about a child."

Damn it, he didn't want her sympathy. He didn't

want her to look at him as a monstrous object of pity and scorn. "Luckily, my sister married and began pushing me down the line of succession quite quickly, so it was a moot point, anyway."

"Where are you now, in the line?"

He stroked Pirate, who had a smile on his smashed, ugly face. "Sixth. Ana is first, followed by her four children."

"So, 'Ana,' your sister whom I talked to, is Anastasia the Nefarious, the Warrior Queen of the Netherlands."

He felt his smile widen. "The Warrior *Crown Princess* of the Netherlands. Our parents are still very much alive."

"And who's after you?" she asked.

"My younger brother Willem and my sister, Margriet. You'll probably meet everyone within a day or so. Ana said that she'll 'arrange something,' which is every bit as ominous as it sounds." He shifted in his seat. "Look, I don't mean for you to be impolite or anything, but when you meet Willem, don't take anything that he says seriously. Margriet is fine. You'll like her."

"Why, is he going to tell me that you're a manwhore who ran around Amsterdam, screwing in all the brothels in the De Wallen district?"

He raised one eyebrow. "I think I liked it better when you only knew about windmills and tulips."

"Yeah. Well. I Googled."

"I never frequented the De Wallen district. Did you find that on the internet?"

"I just read about the red light district. I didn't know that I should Google *you.* If I had, I probably wouldn't be all shocked right now."

"To be clear, Willem might have had such a story planted, if he thought it would be effective or if I would care. He probably would say that or worse if he thought that it would cause me to abdicate."

"Are you serious? Abdicate *what?*"

Ah, such naiveté. "So he could be sixth in line for the throne instead of number seven."

"Why would he want to do that? There would still be your sister and four kids ahead of him!"

Casimir shrugged. "I have no idea why he does anything. The rest of us live in the real world, working in the law or finance or trade. He thinks he's in a high fantasy novel and has to win the throne or die."

"Literally?" she asked, her eyebrows raised and skeptical.

Casimir shrugged. "He's not delusional, but I swear that, if he could have, he would have massacred us all at his wedding last year."

"That is weird, Casimir."

He sighed. "I know."

Rox hesitated, but she asked, "It's actually *Prince* Casimir, isn't it?"

Casimir scratched the cat's chin, knowing that he was being ridiculous, but stroking the cat's fur was soothing. "That's what people will call me to my face in Amsterdam."

Behind his back, they still called him Prince Monster.

Chapter Seventy-Eight

NOTHING CHANGED

Okay, so "Cash Amsberg," Rox's boss, the smokin' hot lawyer whom Rox had known for three, long years, the insufferable tease whom she could make actually giggle when she got on a roll, the man who rescued her from leeches in the Amazon rain forest and gropers in Italy and had poured her into bed on more than one occasion when she misjudged the strength of unfamiliar international liquors, the guy who needed her to rescue him from a persistent Russian prostitute and to hold his hand when he was in pain after the car accident, that guy was actually *Prince* Casimir of the Netherlands.

Rox's head boggled.

She wanted to throttle him.

You need to tell a girl something like that.

But really, nothing had changed.

He was still the same goofball who spoiled her cats. Pirate was currently drooling with contentment on his knee. Seriously, there was a dark spot on Casimir's pants' leg under the cat's chin. He was literally drooling with happiness.

He was still the sharp lawyer whom she worked with, the guy who had torn down a law firm rather than allow their clients to be swindled, and they put on their resting bitch faces together to fence with opposing counsel.

He was still the same guy who could talk to anyone he met, under any circumstances, and have a lively conversation where the other person walked away believing that Casimir was awesome and their new best friend.

That gregariousness and graciousness might have been learned, she realized. Those would be excellent qualities in a royal diplomat, and he had probably been trained as such since he was a little boy.

But Casimir was still the same man.

And Rox was still his same paralegal who was probably the last woman on Earth to sleep with him.

So nothing had really changed.

Other than the fact that Rox really wanted to hide under the table in this private airplane rather than meet his sister, Crown Princess Anastasia the Nefarious, the Warrior Princess who might invade France just for the hell of it.

Chapter Seventy-Nine

CASIMIR'S PLANE

When Arthur's plane landed in London, Rox and Casimir said solemn and refined goodbyes to Maxence and Arthur, who did not nearly kill them by hugging this time, and walked through the jet bridge into the private terminal at Heathrow.

At the end of the tunnel, a squad of commandos in black fatigues swarmed them.

Rox jumped and grabbed Casimir's arm, fully intending to make a run for it, but Casimir laid one arm around her shoulders and then shook the offered hand of one of the commandos. "Excellent to see you again, Lachlan."

The man said something in Dutch and smiled grimly as he shook Casimir's hand.

Casimir spoke Dutch back to him in calm, reassuring tones, and let his hand drop.

The other commandos all faced outward, rifles across their chests and ready.

Rox was not sure how they had managed to get all those guns into England and to brandish them in an airport, but evidently being a royal prince had its perks, like your security didn't have to worry about those pesky gun laws.

The Dutch commando said something again to Casimir, and the whole group moved like one multi-legged beast through the small terminal and to another gate. Rox hurried to keep up.

Wow, the Heathrow private terminal was so big that it had a lot of gates.

The commandos hustled Casimir and Rox down the next tunnel and through the door of a new jet.

Casimir glanced out the windows as they were walking and said something to the Dutch guy whom he had been talking to, but Rox was too busy concentrating on not getting run over by their heavily armed escort to gawk at the plane outside.

She tried to pause in the doorway to take in the huge body of the airplane that yawned in front of her. This airplane was far bigger than Arthur's, a jumbo jet that had been stripped of all its uncomfortable seats for commoners and refitted with living room furniture. Conversation groupings surrounded tables. Part of the way back, a wall divided the plane into another section.

When she stopped, however, Casimir tugged her arm, and the guys behind her still pounded their boots on the gangplank.

She and Casimir sat in one of the wide recliners, and the men who were dressed in black and holding weapons pounded past them toward the rear of the plane.

"It seems that my sister sent the large plane that is usually reserved for state visits. I don't usually travel like this."

"It's good that she cares enough to send the very best." Rox stroked the armrest with one finger. The leather was so soft that it felt like silk bedsheets.

"We're also going to have two fighter jets escort us to The Hague."

"I thought we were going to Amsterdam."

"It seems that the family has decamped to Huis ten Bosch Palace in The Hague, so we'll go there. That's our primary residence anyway."

Rox looked out the porthole window, which seemed larger than normal airplane windows, definitely wider than normal ones. "Is it normal to have fighter jets fly with you everywhere you go?"

"Not at all. It seems that my sister has been watching the news from America and is not amused by the situation."

A terrible thought popped into Rox's head. "Can she forbid you to leave the Netherlands, because she's the princess?"

Casimir laughed. "No. She probably thinks she can, though."

The first commando returned and held out a cell phone. "Her Highness would like to speak with you."

Casimir rolled his eyes and laughed again. "Thank you, Lachlan."

Chapter Eighty

THE HAGUE

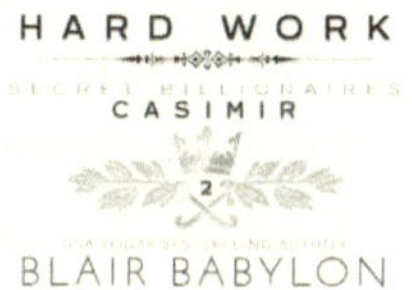

After the royal plane landed in The Hague, an airport shared with the city of Rotterdam, the security guys swung into high gear.

Rox struggled to keep up with Casimir and the battalion of commandos that jogged around them, alert to the crowd's slightest movement as they moved through the airport and to the curb, where a fleet of black limousines was waiting for them.

One of the commandos held open the back door of the second limousine in the line and waved them over.

Casimir grabbed Rox's hand and steadied her as she got into the car. She scooted across the seat, and he folded his long legs to get in behind her. The soldier slammed the door behind them and pounded three times on the roof.

Two more security guys were sitting in the front seat. The one on the passenger side glanced back at her and gave her a tight smile before he resumed scanning the sidewalk and traffic around the car.

The caravan of black limousines drove them into the countryside and into a forest.

A forest. A forest with a castle in it.

Things were weird.

Casimir didn't speak the whole time. He watched the scant traffic and passing trees as if he were waiting for something. When she let her fingers crawl across the leather seat to his hand, he gripped her fingers, but he kept scanning the leafy canopy and other cars, as alert as the commandos in the front seat. The green scent of grass and leaves flowed through the car's vents.

The limo ducked around the large, old-fashioned building to a rear entrance, jolting her backward in the seat.

She just assumed that the building was a hotel. It looked like a hotel, a gorgeous facade and columns and plaster and stuff.

Yep, it looked just like a really nice hotel, one of those that Rox stayed in when she was traveling for work and the law firm was picking up the tab, except that the front didn't have a sign on it.

No Hilton. No Four Seasons. No Holiday Inn.

Yeah, it was a *palace.*

Rox needed to think these things through.

Casimir said to her, "This level of security is highly unusual. I think the firebomb has upset my sister."

The driver said something in Dutch, a dry sarcastic tone lacing his voice.

Casimir chuckled one dry huff. "He said that Ana has been storming around and micromanaging every aspect of the security operation, as she insists on calling it."

The driver said something else, and his low laugh sounded sinister.

Casimir rolled his eyes. "And the gentleman says that we will have a few hours to freshen up before the reception tonight. My parents are out of town, so it will just be my sister, the Crown Princess Anastasia, receiving us."

"We don't have clothes for a reception," Rox protested. "I don't have any clothes at all." She pulled at her tee shirt. "I'm still wearing Brandy's big workout tee shirt because that's the only thing she had that would fit over my," she glanced at the two strangers in the front seat, "chest."

He chuckled. "I'm sure Ana will micromanage that, too."

Ana had, indeed, micromanaged that, too.

They were led through the back door and through gilded hallways to an elevator that opened into a short hallway, kind of like a really nice Manhattan hotel with just three doors on the walls. Casimir walked straight to the one on the end, which didn't have a number or anything on it, and twisted the knob to walk straight inside.

Rox didn't ask him how he knew which one they

would be staying in. She just followed him around like a lost puppy.

Casimir said, "The staff will bring the cats up in a few moments. I heard they had actually found some carriers, so they'll be safer coming up to our apartment."

"This is an apartment?" Rox had been wondering whether she was allowed to sit on the creamy raw silk-upholstered chairs and furniture, and she really hoped that her cats would behave themselves and not sharpen their claws on what must be tens of thousands of dollars' worth of furniture. Or more. She had no idea how to put a value on anything. "I thought this was a hotel."

"This is my apartment for when I'm in town. I keep some clothes here."

All this, thousands of square feet—a living room, a formal dining room that seated ten, two bedrooms, and three bathrooms—just for Casimir to keep a few socks here for the couple of times that he visited. He couldn't visit much. In the last three years, he hadn't taken more than a few weeks of vacation, and most of the time, he had gone to places with beaches.

He said, "I told Ana what your sizes are. She might have already had clothes delivered for you."

When Rox found the other walk-in closet in the bedroom, she found that Ana had indeed had clothes delivered for her and that Ana had exquisite taste. Three little sheath dresses in shades from black to pearly gray hung on one side of the closet, and a gorgeous pink cocktail dress was on the other.

Outside the closet, Casimir called, "She'll have underwear and things in the drawers for you, too."

Rox came out of the closet to find Casimir gathering clothes from drawers and heading toward another door, which she assumed was the bathroom. She asked, "How did *you* know what size I wear?"

"From that time that the airline lost your luggage in New York." He flipped underwear and casual slacks in his hand. "You dragged me shopping with you."

She set her hands on her hips. "You said you wanted to go shopping."

"I didn't want you to have to carry your bags." He raised his eyebrows at her and closed the bathroom door behind himself.

Rox was on her phone, checking her social stuff. Nothing particularly important had happened. She wasn't sure how to write all that had happened during the last day as a social media update or even if she should. The emoticon response would be all over the place.

She was considering understatement: *So, this happened: survived a sniper and firebomb, ended up in the Netherlands, and that guy I work for and am sleeping with might be the King of Holland someday. Selfie!*

A PM from Brandy read: *All right, who the hell are*

Arthur and Maxence? We just got donations that will keep the shelter afloat for five years.

She was beginning to kind of like those guys.

Casimir set the phone back in its cradle and kept his hand on it. "Willem is coming up for a few minutes to talk."

"Isn't he the one who wants to be the king?"

She replayed that sentence in her mind. *Absurd.* How did a nice little Southern girl like herself end up in The Hague, casually commenting on court intrigues?

OMG, court intrigues. She had to work that into her post somehow.

"Yes. My younger brother." Casimir said that softly, thoughtfully.

She set the phone down. "He isn't coming up with assassins to kill you, is he?"

Casimir's eyebrows twitched down, and he didn't smile. "Probably not."

"You're kidding around, right?"

"Ana has security personnel in the hallway. Willem might be many things, but he isn't stupid."

"Oh. Right. I feel all kinds of better, then. Does he have a British accent like you or a Dutch accent like Ana?"

Casimir glanced at her. "You picked that up, did you?"

She shrugged. "It's pretty obvious."

"My brother and sisters grew up together here in Amsterdam and The Hague, so they speak English with a Dutch accent. I grew up at Le Rosey boarding school in Switzerland, where I learned English from a British tutor."

She had wondered how that had worked, how Casimir had met Arthur and Maxence at the Swiss boarding school, but he was Dutch. "I can't believe your parents sent you away."

"It was for the best. Maxence and I had already been friends since before the car accident. Once I got to Le Rosey, he and Arthur became my brothers."

"I could never send my children to boarding school."

"The press was hounding me. My parents had to get me away from them, and some of the family situation was not ideal."

Whoa. That was interesting. He had never mentioned anything about a family situation before. "I can't imagine boarding school was better than living at home."

"It was a great deal better. Within two weeks, I stopped flinching every time a bush rustled. Within a few months, I was much happier. It was definitely the best decision to get me out of the Netherlands."

She glanced up at him, but he was still staring straight ahead.

"Ana and I are close because we were children together before I was sent away when I was seven. I barely know Margriet. She was a toddler when I left."

"And Willem?"

His mouth was set in a grim line. "He's two years younger than I am. We were never close."

The door rattled as someone knocked on it.

"That was quick," Casimir muttered. More loudly, "Come in!"

On the other side of the living room, the door opened, and a man entered.

The new guy was tall, Rox could tell by the fact that he was still an imposing presence even when walking through the oversized door, and he had bright blond hair that glistened in the sunlight streaming through the windows. Even from across the room, he looked like Casimir.

A *lot* like him.

Rox glanced up at Casimir, who stood rock-still by her side. He didn't so much as blink.

The man called from across the room, "Casimir!"

His voice sounded like Casimir's.

Beside her, Casimir straightened, and his stony expression turned into the one that she knew was his resting bitch face modified with a formal smile.

That was odd. Casimir only used that face during negotiations with very unpleasant opposing counsel. One time, the other lawyer had been chewing tobacco and spitting the chew juice into a paper cup that soaked through pretty quickly. Brown liquid had dribbled down the side of the cup, and a ring of sour spit had bubbled up on the table, which had seeped onto the corner of the contract that they were debating. The lawyer had handed

Casimir the chew-stained contract to look at a particular clause, and Casimir had worn that tight, bland smile the whole time he was holding the soggy paper.

As the other man came closer, Rox could see that he really did look a lot like Casimir—meaning that he was drop-dead gorgeous, with strong cheekbones and a square jaw that would turn every woman's head in a room to look at him—*just* like him, except for the new guy's blond hair and the fact that his eyes were a pale shade of blue.

They looked as alike as the best plastic surgeons in the world could have made them.

The smile on the other guy's face was wide and genuine, and he held his hand extended as he walked across the room. "Casimir! When did you get in? I didn't even know that you were coming home."

"It was an unplanned trip," Casimir said, shaking his hand. "May I present Roxanne Neil, my very dear friend with whom I have worked at the law office in California for three years now. Rox, this is my brother Willem."

Rox shook his hand. It was an ordinary, firm handshake. His palm was warm and dry, and he smiled a gorgeous smile at her. "A pleasure to meet you, Ms. Neil."

"Call me Rox," she said. "Pleased to meet you."

It was like Casimir had a blonder twin.

Bad thoughts about Casimir and his almost-twin brother in her bed rose in her mind. If anything in the world was sexier than Casimir, it was two Casimirs.

Casimiruses.

Casimiri.

Something like that.

Willem turned back to talk to Casimir. "Good Lord, what did you do to your face now?"

He shrugged, his form-fitting suit moving with his body. "Bit of a car accident. Slight problem with a fire."

"You should have that looked at. You'll have the press crawling on us all over again." He turned to Rox, a warm and amused smile on his face. "They would not leave us alone when he was a child. When he was out with us, the press swarmed all of us. You couldn't even walk without one of them tripping you."

"That must've been terrible for you," Rox said, trying not to let one eyebrow rise.

Casimir said, "I was planning to have it looked at."

"Sooner rather than later, I suppose. I can't believe that Ana is scheduling a reception for you while you look like that. You'll wear a bandage or a mask of some sort, of course."

Oh, that was going too far.

Rox stood a little straighter. "I like it."

They both looked down at her, two tall, glorious man-gods staring down from the heavens.

She said, "I think he looks manly. It's just a little scratch, and it gives his face character. It makes him look different than all the other pretty boys out there. I have problems telling those guys apart."

A hint of a smile curved Casimir's mouth, but Willem frowned. "Of course he shouldn't leave it like *that.* He needs to get it fixed."

"Nope." She looked right into Casimir's brilliant green eyes. "I think he looks *better.* I think it's *sexy.*"

Casimir watched her, that small, real smile still playing around his mouth.

Willem's frown deepened. "He can't look like *that* when he's representing the Kingdom of the Netherlands at official functions."

Rox grinned. "Sure, he can. He has stories to tell about it. People will relate to him better. And I wouldn't have him change a thing."

Casimir's eyes softened. His hand by his side twitched as if he had almost reached to take her hand but couldn't.

Willem said, "I think it's disgraceful. Casimir, it's revolting. How will you ever marry someone of importance looking like that? What would the people say if, God forbid, anything were to happen to Ana and her children and *you* took the throne? There would be riots in the streets if Prince Monster were the king."

Rox was already swinging her fist at his stomach when Casimir caught her arm. *"You asshole!"*

"Now, Rox," Casimir said, "violence never solved anything." He sounded far too calm.

Willem watched her, his arms crossed.

She shook her arm, trying to make Casimir let her go. *"I will punch that slimeball right in the kisser."*

"She's got a temper," Casimir told his brother. "Perhaps we should continue this discussion some other time."

"Oh, I'm riled up all the way past angry-Southern-girl level and about to go *biblical* on him!"

Casimir laughed. "Run, Willem."

Willem rolled his eyes, clearly annoyed at her plebeian outburst. "I'll see you later, *Casimir.*"

That last word was barbed, expressing his disdain for the commoner.

The commoner who was going to tear his face off. "You come back here and I'll beat your fancy ass! Someone should have whupped you more often to learn you some manners!"

Willem's last look at Casimir spoke volumes of disapproval, and he strolled out the door.

She snarled, "You let me go and I will make sure that he's never that impolite to anyone again!"

Casimir pulled her into his arms and held her, his cheek pressed against her hair. "You really can't threaten to 'whup' members of the royal family. The security staff will look askance."

"Seriously, you're not going to have a temper tantrum over that?"

"Not here."

"I—*really?*"

"Never."

"If we were in the office and someone spoke to you like that, you would have *a proper rant,*" she made fun of his British accent there, "and chew his butt a new one."

He stroked her back. "Besides, I don't need to. As always, you've taken care of the situation for me. I'll just sign off on it."

"You're weird here. I can hardly wait to get you back to the States."

He bent, and Rox felt him press his cheek to her hair. "Me, too."

She wrapped her arms around his chest and squeezed. "I *will* whup his ass. What a jackass."

As she had often heard growing up in the South, evil wears a beautiful face.

Chapter Eighty-One

PRINCESS ANASTASIA THE NEFARIOUS

HARD WORK

CASIMIR

BLAIR BABYLON

Rox fidgeted with her dress. The pale pink formal dress fit her beautifully. Casimir's sister had even supplied pantyhose and shoes that fit her, somehow perfectly. A woman had arrived to do her make-up and hair, all of which felt exceedingly unnatural.

It was like the Crown Princess of the Netherlands was actually a fairy godmother.

They waited outside huge doors. Two men dressed in royal blue and orange livery, which meant really old-fashioned servant-clothes, faced each other and would open the doors for them in just a few minutes.

Beyond the doors, Rox could hear a crowd muttering and a string quartet playing.

She asked, "Can't we just meet Ana in your apartment or something?"

Casimir shook his head. "If we were going to be

here longer, we probably could have an informal meeting and then do a formal presentation later, but I'm hoping that we can leave within a few days. Maybe we could meet one of my parents at some point, but I think you'll like Ana better."

He was wearing full evening dress—a black tuxedo with a white vest and tie—which was just so much more formal than she had ever seen him before. Cash wore finely cut business suits to work, of course, and he dressed in a black-tie tux for the annual Holiday Formal soiree that the law firm threw every year, which really made all the admins and paralegals swoon. It was like he was advertising for them to get in line for the next year's harvest.

But Casimir in a white-tie tux, tails, and an orange and blue sash with medals even made stone-cold Rox's heart go all aflutter. *Damn.*

Rox slid her fingers into his hand. "You really don't like it here, do you?"

"I'm more comfortable elsewhere."

"I'm sorry. I wish I could hug you but I'm sure that the protocol guy would come back here and admonish me again. He sure didn't like the way I curtsy, and I learned that at Cotillion."

He squeezed her hand. "It should only take a few minutes."

The footmen set their feet against the floor and leaned back to open the towering doors.

Contrasting colognes rode the air currents to where they stood: rose and lily and sandalwood, and her nose burned, confused by all the scents.

Rox followed Casimir as he walked from the enormous, cavernous waiting room where they had been standing into an even larger, grander room with ceilings that floated so high above them that Rox had to squint to see the delicate frescoes painted all the way up there among the arches and carved crown moldings. Every square inch of the formal room had been fitted with paintings, even up the arches and on the sides of niches.

And the ceiling! It had to be at least four stories up there. Maybe five. Possibly *six*. Chandeliers hung from wires and blazed with silver light like candles and sparklers hovering in the sky. Rox couldn't even figure out the perspective, and she felt squished and tiny in the towering room.

High ceilings.

Oh. My. God.

This was what Arthur and Maxence had been joking about when they had said that Casimir knew a lot about places with *high ceilings.* They hadn't meant sex clubs like The Devilhouse.

They had meant that Casimir had been raised in a royal *palace.*

Now she felt like an idiot.

That sensation was becoming ridiculously familiar.

The crowd moved aside like a yellow brick road parting the poppies, forming a path to a woman standing on a dais in front of a tall, tall chair, twenty feet high, that had a crown hanging over it like a wall teester that held curtains draping over a bed.

The slim, white woman stood in front of the throne, the light from the chandeliers shining all around her, dressed in a pale blue formal dress that precisely reached her toes.

Diamonds glittered in her golden hair.

Rox lost her breath and hesitated. If Casimir had gone on without her, she would have turned and fled, but when she stopped, he stopped.

He turned back and held out his hand.

Okay, so she had to do this with him.

Meeting the family was always nerve-wracking.

She took his hand and walked down the path of people on the actual red carpet trail toward the dais, the throne, and the Crown Princess. After a second, he dropped his hand from hers but touched her back, a calming gesture that was somehow less PDA than holding hands but was, if anything, more possessive.

She liked it, and her shoulders lowered farther. She wished she could lean into him, but the whole crowd was watching her walk, their glistening eyes following her every step in that long, beaded dress that reached her toes.

A man wearing a black suit—which was a relief after all the guys playing dress-up in medieval garb like this was a freaking Renaissance Fair—held a piece of paper and announced their names.

Casimir bowed his head, but the protocol droid, er, *guy*, had told her to curtsy deeply here, fussing that her curtsy was neither deep nor subservient enough.

Rox did her best to bend her knee and not fall on her face, mostly succeeding, she thought.

The Crown Princess Anastasia, who looked about thirty-three-ish and indeed was as beautiful as she was evil, walked down the steps of the dais and held Rox's shoulders. She whispered, "Up, now."

Rox stood up, managing to bobble only a little in the high heels and slim skirt, a deadly combination. It was a good thing that she had worn skirt suits to work for years and was used to dealing with balance issues.

Anastasia kept her hands on Rox's shoulders, leaned in, and *hugged her.*

The crowd pitter-pat applauded.

Rox backed up and almost stumbled when her heel caught her skirt hem.

The Crown Princess Anastasia said, "It is a pleasure to meet you, Ms. Neil."

"And you—ma'am. Please call me Rox."

"Excellent. Please call me Ana." She turned to Casimir and shook his hand heartily. "So you warned her about us?" Ana asked him.

"Oh, certainly." Casimir paused. "Most of it."

"And you told her that I'm nefarious and evil and will summarily execute her if she offends me?"

His small smile reached his brilliant green eyes. "Absolutely. I told her that part first."

"Oh, good. I hate that surprised look on people's faces when I order their beheading. It's so distasteful."

My God. She had Casimir's dry sense of humor.

Rox smiled.

They were going to get along just fine.

Chapter Eighty-Two

THE ORANGE HALL AT HUIS TEN BOSCH PALACE

HARD WORK
CASIMIR
BLAIR BABYLON

The reception lasted until long after midnight, dining and dancing and talking with dozens of new people. Rox fretted about remembering all their names.

When Casimir noticed that she was repeating everyone's name at least three times in conversation, he whispered to her not to worry about filing them away. If they had an important meeting with any of these people, admins would prep them. She should relax and enjoy the evening.

So she did.

She caught him smiling at her several times throughout the night and a lot while they were dancing.

Everyone seemed fine with Casimir, talking and laughing with him. Indeed, they seemed a little more helpful, a little extra kind, and eager to make an introduction for him or get his opinion on something.

They were all one notch too loud and jovial.

Casimir returned the pleasantries, smiling that elegant smile of his that made his green eyes seem more kind than sparkling, listening to what they said, shaking hands or inclining his head when someone curtsied, but he seemed just a little more reserved than in California, a little more private.

A little more shielded.

When Rox looked back, though, catching people out of the corner of her eye after they thought that she and Casimir had turned away, a lot of people glanced at the floor, something like shame or regret passing over their faces for the brief pause before they turned to greet the next person.

Rox watched them more closely, her instincts finely honed by years of evaluating the legal shenanigans and manipulations by unscrupulous lawyers.

Yeah, they might like Casimir, and they might want him to like them, but there was an undercurrent of a past or other issues between them.

No wonder Casimir didn't like it here. In California, he could be himself, open and honest and ethical and laughing and everyone's friend.

Here, he was haunted by Prince Monster.

She saw Willem working the crowd a little ways away from them, and she watched him.

Most of the guests greeted Willem with pleasure, speaking with animation, and walked away smiling, oblivious to what he was. A few people seemed thrilled to see him, pumping his hand and exclaiming, but when he turned away, they swallowed hard or wiped their palms on their thighs. Rox actually saw one of the women shudder, ripples cascading down the silvery beaded fringe glittering on her dress. Others were merely reserved, cordial, but made their escape as soon as propriety allowed.

Sometimes, when Willem thought no one was looking, his icy glance over the crowd or at a certain person or two made Rox clutch her drink more tightly. He was really a lizard, cold-blooded and inexorably crawling through the crowd toward them.

And getting closer.

Rox said to Casimir, “Let’s dance,” and they walked out onto the center floor to waltz to the small orchestra that had set up at the back of the room after the supper. His strong arms settled around her, and Rox practically melted with relief.

While they were dancing, Casimir said, “You fit in here extraordinarily well.”

“Oh no, I don’t,” she protested, following his very firm lead. “I have been concentrating on not falling off my pumps or snagging my hem with my heels all night long. The silk in this dress is so delicate that it would just rip right off of me and expose my control-top panty hose for all the world to see. And there are so many *people.*” *One*-two-three, *one*-two-three, she counted in her head while she talked. “And they’ve all got titles and beauty pageant sashes and tiaras and the guys are wearing man-jewelry like yourself, there.” She touched the white cross medal-thing that hung on a ribbon around his neck. A lion reared up in the center, extending its claws, just like his tattoo on his right forearm. "And they're all milling around. And they all know each other. I have been hanging on you all night like a howler monkey in a sidecar."

He was laughing by the time she finished her complaint.

And now she felt like a petulant little whiner for throwing shade upon the royal reception that his lovely sister had thrown on a few hours' notice.

She plastered a weak smile on her face. "But I like it!"

He laughed more. "I'm glad that you like it."

"What is all this?" she asked, poking the brooch on the left side of his chest. The eight-pointed silver starburst surrounded a gold-enameled lion, and gold letters spelling out "Je maintiendrai" arched above the lion. His beauty-pageant sash was orangey-gold with blue stripes on the edges.

"It's a thing that we wear."

"Baloney. It means something."

"It really doesn't. It's a House Order, called the Order of the Gold Lion of the House of Nassau. It was awarded to me when I was born, so it doesn't mean anything. It isn't a medal for bravery or for service. It was just handed to me because I was born to a particular set of parents."

The medal dangling under his white bow-tie had the same lion on the same blue circle, but the cross was one of those eight-pointed Germanic-looking designs, a Maltese Cross. "It might seem useless and meaningless to you because you didn't do anything to earn it, but it's pretty."

"I think that sums up my opinion of the monarchy."

Okay, then. She stepped and turned with him as the waltz music swelled and the other dancers swung around them.

He held her hands more firmly. "You waltz beautifully. Why haven't we danced before?"

"Because we travel together for work. You don't go *dancing* when you travel together for work."

"We go dancing all the time when we travel."

"Only when the other side insists on taking us, but we never *waltz.*"

"I would have, if I had thought that you wouldn't have backhanded me and told me to 'keep my paws to myself.'"

She laughed at his ear-curling hodge-podge of a British accent and a Southern one. "Exactly."

He said, "I didn't even know you could waltz."

"Cotillion, again. I was one of those prissy little Southern girls who dreamed of their debut from the time they were seven, when they are presented to society as a debutante wearing a white ball gown with crinolines and hoops like Scarlett O'Hara and opera-length white gloves. For that one, brief, shining night, we show off that we could be proper upper-class, decorative wives without a thought in our heads, that we can waltz, foxtrot, and do several other useless dances, and that we can select the shrimp fork out of five or more other stupid forks. And then next Monday we go back to high school and go on with our lives as if nothing ever happened. Because it didn't. It's all fluff and noise."

Casimir was still smiling down at her. "I like the thoughts in your head."

She shot a wicked glance up at him, a flirtatious smirk. "I like the thoughts in your head, too."

His eyes brightened, and his hand around her waist pulled her a few inches closer to himself.

THE GARDEN BY MOONLIGHT

A few hours later, well after Rox's phone battery had died sometime around one o'clock and most of the guests were gone, Casimir led her outside to the gardens, a real garden around the real royal palace in the woods, telling her that he wanted to show her a thing back in there.

You know, a thing.

In the garden of a royal palace.

The palace where Casimir had grown up.

Things were weird.

They walked, first arm-in-arm, and then he slid his arm around her waist. She wrapped her arm around his middle, too, feeling his belt and trim middle under her fingers.

Rox stumbled on the dim walkway, laughing and giddy and slightly tipsy. The waiters had been pushing the champagne, swapping her empty glass for a full one before she had a chance to tell them that she'd had enough.

Then one waitress had discovered that Rox liked the harder stuff and, evidently, had made it her mission to introduce Rox to Dutch liquors or get her totally wasted in public, she wasn't sure which.

Solar lights illuminated the edges of the path under their feet and the pale flowers along the sides, but darkness clung to the branches of the tall trees around them.

"It's those foreign liquors again," she told Casimir, "I cannot judge how strong a drink is with those foreign liquors in it. Give me a good ol' Jack and Coke, and this never happens."

He was laughing, too, his body limber and relaxed against her side. "I can't remember when I've had such a good time at an official function."

She was pressed so tightly against his body that she felt his phone buzz in his pants' pocket, a flicker through the heavy beads shimmering on her dress. "That's because you're hanging out with all those old fuddy-duddies. You just need to get down and get funky with your fine self."

He was laughing so hard that he was almost stumbling, but he kept his arm around her waist and lifted her every time she dragged a heel across the rough stones in the walkway.

Because her head was totally spinning. *Totally.*

He led her down paths edged with hedges and paths without, past wide, dark lawns and under trees and by gurgling fountains.

His phone buzzed again in his pocket, tickling her.

She stepped sideways, but he tugged her back under his arm. "Come on, I want to show you this."

At the end of the path, after a short walk punctuated by Casimir's phone shivering through his pants against her, a small gazebo rose out of the foliage, white wood lattice overgrown with ivy and fall flowers.

Casimir took out his cell phone and turned the flashlight app on. A beacon of light sprayed from the phone, and he laid it on the little bench inside, lighting up the flowers hanging from the arches overhead.

"This is beautiful," Rox said, wandering around the small structure. She grazed the flowers and leaves with her fingertips, and they swayed where she had touched them.

When she turned, he was watching her, his hands tucked in his pockets.

On the bench, his phone vibrated again, rattling on the wood and jittering the light that shone on the leaves and vines.

He said, "When I was a kid, very young, this was my haven. With the way that door faces the hidden path, the photographers couldn't get a picture through the trees, even though they hid in the forest with telephoto lenses. For about six months, I came here every day for at least a few hours until one of the nannies came to retrieve me. You would think that they would have started looking here when I was missing, but I think they were giving me time alone. It was the only place outside where I could get away from them. I was all right inside the palace, of course, but no child wants to stay inside all day."

The gazebo walls seemed closer, and the roof, lower, as Casimir described his hiding spot. Rox came back over to him and touched his arm.

The phone buzzed on the bench again.

Casimir wrapped her hand under his arm and led her to the bench. "Sit for a moment."

"Thank you." Sore spots ringed her feet where the new shoes had rubbed her. A blister was forming on her heel, a needlestick of pain, but she hadn't wanted to stop dancing, either. She pried her shoes off with her toes, and her feet felt like they ballooned two sizes as soon as the high-heeled pumps flopped onto the cobblestones. Oh, her *toes,* her poor, broken, blistered *toes.*

Casimir sank to one knee in front of her and held both her hands in his.

Oh, that's right. They had some unfinished business that had been so rudely interrupted by a flippin' firebomb.

He started, "Roxanne Dolly Neil—"

"Yes," Rox said.

He frowned. "I beg your pardon?"

"Yes," she said again. What, was that the wrong answer in this situation?

He frowned, lines gathering shadows on his forehead in the dim light. "You didn't even hear what I was going to ask."

"There're only three occasions in a girl's life when you hear all three of your names: when you are in deep trouble with your momma, when you are being served a warrant for your arrest, and when someone is proposing marriage to you. So, *yes.*"

"I might have been going to ask if you wanted to get a taco at one of the all-night food trucks down by the bars," he insisted, his brilliant green eyes sparkling with laughter by the column of light from the cell phone.

The phone behind her vibrated again, shivering the bench under her legs.

She said, "You weren't going to ask me if I wanted a taco, and you know it."

"Perhaps I was going to serve a warrant for threatening the life of a member of the royal family."

She thought about it and frowned. "I haven't threatened to kill you lately."

"I meant Willem."

She pointed back toward the palace and the reception. "I saw how those people in there were looking at him. No court would convict me. Now you stop teasing me."

"All right. I won't tease you. Yes, marry me, *lieveke.* Always be my paralegal whom I can't do without and my wife."

"That's going to be in our vows, that you aren't allowed to tease me."

"Then you'll have to say 'obey.'"

"I beg your pardon you son of a—"

"Kidding! I'm kidding you. I can barely get you to make me a cup of coffee when we're in the office."

"I am a licensed paralegal, not a naughty secretary. The *only* time that I made you a cup of coffee was that one time when you came in the office with a hundred and two-degree temperature and the shakes from the flu because we were meeting with Pitt-Jolie's people that morning."

He looked at her from the sides of his eyes, his mouth turning down. "You didn't actually say yes yet. The stones are beginning to grate on my knee."

"What? I said yes. At least twice. Why are you still down there?"

"But that was before I finished my—"

"Get up! Get up!"

"—sentence."

She tugged on his shoulders. "Come on. *Yes.* I said yes. Now *get up.*"

He reached into his pocket and pulled out something that glowed in the dim light of the cell phone that was buzzing yet again.

White diamonds surrounded a dark and brilliantly green rectangular stone. The gold band curved down into his fingertips.

"Oh, my," she said and held out her left hand.

He slipped it onto her ring finger. The size was a little jiggly, if anything. "If you don't like it, we can select another from the collection here or go to Paris for a few days and have one made."

She looked up from the emerald and the ring into Casimir's dark green, sparkling eyes. "I like this one."

He slid onto the bench beside her and wrapped

her in his arms, his mouth finding hers in the dim light from the cell phone. Even bickering, even teasing, she melted against his rugged body and slid her arms around his waist. His hand pressed along her curves, holding her.

His voice lowered, "Have you ever been made love to in a royal palace before?"

"No. Have you?"

"I probably shouldn't answer that question. You think that I'm enough of a manslut as it is."

"You're right. I don't want to know. *Ever.* Have you ever *done it* in this gazebo before?"

She felt his intake of breath against her, and he looked off to the side, as if he expected reporters or his sister to walk into the gazebo. "No."

"Oooh. It's like you're a virgin. That's hot." She slid her hand down his back and grabbed his ass. "It's like I'm taking advantage of the hot, young prince."

"I'm two years older than you are."

"Shush, my sweet, young prince. Let me show you the ways of wicked women."

"And you have done the deed before in the garden of a royal palace?" he asked, his lips brushing her neck right in that soft place behind her jaw.

"Hey, you're the blushing innocent, here. It doesn't matter what I have or haven't done."

"I take that to mean that you haven't."

"Like I said, you're the sweet, young thing, here, and I'm going to have you in this garden, out here, where anyone might walk in or see us through the leaves."

Under her hands, she felt the shiver run through him, and he scraped his teeth over her neck and pulled aside the thin strap of her dress to lip her shoulder, blowing his warm breath over her skin.

Rox hiked her skirt up around her thighs and straddled the bench, turning Casimir so that he did the same. In the laser-like flashlight beam from the cell phone, shadows cut his face into a patchwork of darkness and pale skin, and she could see the scar on his cheek and his brilliant green eyes.

She stood on one foot and with one knee on the bench so that she was taller than he was where he was sitting. She kissed him, her hands on his face and her fingers feeling the satiny smoothness of his jaw in her palms.

With his face turned upward like that, under her lips, it almost did feel like he was the inexperienced one, except that no inexperienced man kissed like that. His lips caressed and sucked hers, and his hands circled her waist, touching her sides and ribs. His hands were so large that his fingers almost touched each other over her spine, even though Rox's waist was as ample as the rest of her.

Her fingers trailed down while she kissed him, holding his shoulder with one hand but still keeping her other hand on his left cheek. Her thumb grazed the scar there, and Casimir sucked in a breath.

"Did I hurt you?" she asked.

"No."

It must've just startled him when she had touched the scar.

She ran her thumb over the lower part of the scar again, keeping well away from where the ember had burned him.

This time, she definitely felt him tense against her.

"Don't," he said.

"I am going to touch every part of you: your mouth," she kissed him hard, breaching his lips and tangling her tongue with his, "and your body," she ran her hands down his chest and ribs, feeling the hard ripples and sinews under his clothes, "and every inch of your skin."

She kissed her way over his jaw and pulled his collar aside to nip his neck.

Casimir stretched under her mouth and hands, and a thrill ran through her as his fingers tightened on her hips. She pushed his black tuxedo jacket off his broad shoulders and down his biceps and arms. It fell on the bench behind him, the long tails trailing down into the darkness at their feet.

She trailed her lips up over his jaw and found the place on his cheek where his skin twisted under her lips. Careful not to get anywhere near the burned area that was blistered, Rox ran her lips over the healed scar tissue.

Casimir was still tense in her arms, but Rox knew how to distract him from that. Her fingers found his belt, and she unbuckled it.

He leaned back, bracing himself with his arms

on the bench behind him, and glanced down at her hands.

Yeah, she had his full attention now.

She unfastened his pants and pulled his shirts out so she could reach her hand inside. Under her fingers, through his underwear, he was already hard, his erection curving back toward his stomach.

He groaned when she touched him.

Casimir pushed himself off the bench behind him and grabbed her around her waist, his hands sliding up to find her breasts. He kissed the tops of them, and a moment of worry passed through her about his mouth staining the silk, but he slid his thumbs over the thin fabric, kissing her neck and where she swelled above the neckline, caressing her until she was panting and her nipples were tight.

His hands roamed her body, and he drew her down, pressing on her hips, to kiss her mouth again.

Rox rose back up to cover his mouth with hers, kissing him, while he groped her hips and her ass and her thighs, sliding his hands under the thin silk of the dress. His hands rose farther, finding the waist of her control-top pantyhose, and he stripped them down her legs.

She stepped to the side of the bench and helped him drag the hose off her ankles. His fingers were already up inside her dress again near her waist, and he snagged the waistband of her panties and let those drop around her feet, too.

As soon as she was bare, he reached for her, digging his fingers into the soft flesh of her hips first, and then sliding his hand around and underneath her. His fingers caressed her folds, every massage sending delicious shudders through her.

Rox arched backward, her head falling back as he rubbed her first outside, then deeper, then finally slipping inside her.

He whispered, "God, you're so wet. You're always so wet for me."

She had been for three years.

He rubbed her harder, rougher, sliding inside of her and out on her slippery skin.

Every slip of his fingers was winding her more tightly, and her fingernails bit into his shirt over his shoulders.

"Come for me," he said. "Come now."

Not yet.

Rox shoved his shoulders, and Casimir toppled backwards on the bench. She tugged and pulled away his clothes, exposing his cock.

Her voice was harsh in her throat. "Do you have a condom?"

"No." He didn't even open his teeth when he spoke.

"You okay with that?"

"Hell, yes."

She moved up him, crawling, and Casimir reached between them to angle his cock to nudge against her center. The light from the cell phone's beacon shone from behind her, and her shadow lay over Casimir's white tuxedo shirt and the sash that still hung from his right shoulder. The pale light touched his face, shining from below his chin. Odd shadows deepened the scar on his left cheek, and slivers of light highlighted his cheekbones.

She pushed herself down on him, wrapping her body around him as she took him inside of her.

His lips parted as his brilliant green eyes glazed over.

Rox had all of him now, all of him inside of her, and she moved on his body, tilting her hips as she swayed on him.

Casimir bit his lip, and his fingers clutched her thighs. For a moment, it looked like he was going to lose control right then, but he gasped a deep breath and pushed himself up on the bench to half-sitting.

Rox straightened, her feet planted on the ground on either side of him and the low bench, raising herself up with her legs and lowering herself back down onto him. He watched between them for a moment, where their bodies connected, and she felt the air leave his body as if he had been punched. She swiveled her hips as she took him inside her, almost like she was dancing above him.

When he turned his face up to her, his eyes hooded, Rox leaned down and kissed him, and she continued to stroke him with her body.

He wrapped his arms around her waist and shoved her down onto him, the side of his face pressed against her shoulder as he thrust inside her.

His urgency startled her, but his deep thrusts rubbed her inside and shoved against her clit. She grabbed his shoulders, her cheek pressed against his, holding on as he stroked into her. Her body tightened, and her breath quickened. Between her thighs, his body felt like cords of steel were wound around his flesh, and she held on as his every leap up into her spiraled her toward release.

The tension clenched harder around her, and she was keening between her clenched teeth. Casimir leaned her back and pushed harder into her, filling her so deeply and grinding against her so that the knot inside her broke, throbbing through her veins and her muscles, all the way up to her head and the world went white and silent and fiery.

She drifted amid the roaring silence.

His arms.

She was in his arms, clutching his neck, while they both tried to breathe. His forehead was resting against her shoulder, his breath warm on her skin and trickling down her, cooling the sweat on her breasts.

He pressed his lips to her shoulder. "*Lieveke,* marry me."

"Yes," she said. "I will. Yes, Casimir."

His arms tightened around her, "Every time I think that I couldn't possibly love you more, you take my breath away."

She stroked the short hair above the back of his neck. "I love you, too."

"I love you." He kissed her shoulder. "*Mijn lieveke, ik hou van jou.*"

Rox didn't need a translation. She just curled her body in his arms and held on.

In time, with care, they unwound themselves and, still touching each other's face and hands, arranged their clothes so that they weren't completely scandalous.

Her pantyhose still lay in a heap on the stones. It felt too good to have them off, so she didn't bother with struggling back into them.

They sat side-by-side on the bench. Casimir had his arm around her as she huddled next to him, and they watched the leaves sway in the little breeze by the light of his cell phone.

"I can't believe that we didn't use a condom again." Rox was a little mortified. "It won't happen again. I'll go on the Pill or something. We can't keep playing roulette like this."

He kissed her hair again. "Don't."

"Don't what?" she asked, still watching the leaves sway.

"You want something that I've never done before? I've never had sex without a condom before you. I've never wanted to make a woman pregnant with my child. I've never been a father. I've never tried to. I've never wanted to." She looked up at him, and in the night, his green eyes seemed softer. He smiled but bit his lip. "You're my first."

A lump hardened in her throat. "You're my first, too."

He adjusted his arms around her and leaned his head back. "I wonder what he would look like."

"She," she corrected him. "Our first would be a she."

"First, huh? Of how many?"

"Couple, maybe. I'm an only. It's not all it's cracked up to be."

"I'm not an only. I can't recommend parts of that, either."

"Your sister seems nice."

"Crown Princess Ana the Nefarious would have you drawn and quartered for saying that."

"I'll take my chances."

"Ana is sweet, but don't tell her I said that."

"What does she call you?"

"Casimir."

"You mean she doesn't have a pet name for you, like Ana the Nefarious?"

He sighed. "Casimir the Notorious."

"I like that a lot better than Prince Monster."

Beside her, he stiffened. "Where did you hear that?"

Oops. Crap. "I asked Maxence about some things."

"Why didn't you ask me?"

"I didn't want to dredge anything up. I just needed to know some things, and I didn't want to upset you by asking."

"I'm not so easily upset as that. You can ask me things."

She trailed a finger over the ribbon that lay across his chest, now crushed and wrinkled. "Okay, how many kids do you want to have?"

He chuckled. "See? I'm not so easily upset. Perhaps seven."

Terror gripped her, and she leaned away from him to run the hell away. *"Are you serious?"*

"I think Ana is going for six, so we could beat her by one. Or two. Maybe we should have *eight.*"

"You can't be serious."

"I might be teasing you, but wouldn't you like to have all those little counts and countesses running about?"

Rox paused. "Counts and countesses? Not princes and princesses?"

"Assuming that everything stays in place, they would be counts and countesses. Otherwise everyone in the Netherlands would be a prince or princess by now."

"I don't know, man. Sounds like a deal-breaker to me."

He laughed and jostled her with his arm. "I think this evening has completely changed my impression of this gazebo."

She watched the light and shadows flutter among the leaves, and when she held her hand up, the spray of light from his cell phone behind him on the bench caught in the huge emerald on her engagement ring.

"I really like the ring," she said, admiring it on her finger and turning her hand to catch the light better. "It was a good choice."

"Everybody does sapphires these days, ever since Wills and Kate, and really ever since Diana."

"It's weird that you're on a first name basis with those guys. Those guys William and Kate. My good buddies Barack and Michelle. My dudes Beyoncé and Jay Z." *Wait a minute. Casimir was a freakin' prince.* "Have you *met* them?"

"Well, yes, if you mean Wills and Kate. Not the other people. I see them at most social events. I think Wills is my seventh cousin, if I remember correctly. Maybe eighth."

"I know that all you royals are as inbred as a hoarder's housecat, but seriously? You're related to *them?*"

He shrugged, obviously uncomfortable. "Through William the Fourth of the Netherlands, a common ancestor, and Anna of Hannover who was the daughter of George II of Great Britain."

"So you actually know them. Duchess Kate and Prince William, the Duke and Duchess of Cambridge. You know, those guys. You *know* them."

Casimir looked down at their hands, still clasped on his knees. "I was at their wedding."

"I would have seen you on television!"

"It was before we met."

"Oh, my God. I have to find my disk and see if I can spot you."

"I was in the middle of the crowd, but the cameras caught me and Ana a few times. You can meet them when they come to our wedding."

Her hands flew up in the air, fingers splayed wide. "Really? Oh, my God." She fanned herself. "*No.* Really? *No.* You're messing with me. *You are teasing me again!*"

He laughed. "If they're free, they probably will."

"Oh, wow." Yeah, *all* his family would have to be invited. "Does Willem have to come?"

"My brother must be invited. Protocol."

"Can the invitation be addressed wrong? That works sometimes."

Casimir laughed. "We'll plan it tomorrow. Arthur and Maxence will stand up with me, of course. You?"

"Brandy, if she can get away. She has a lot going on."

Beside her cheek, Casimir's chest shook with laughter.

She knew exactly what he was chuckling at. "Oh, stop."

"Who else? Your father? People from the office? Other friends?"

"All that. I'll put together a list." She let her head rest against his chest.

Beyond the leaves shingling the gazebo, pale pink strands of light glimmered in the air.

She asked, "You were kidding about eight kids, right?"

"I was thinking somewhere around two to four, with discussion, assuming everything works out."

"That sounds not quite so insane."

She leaned against his shoulder, feeling his arms around her in the dark.

That damn cell phone buzzed the bench yet again.

"What on Earth is going on with your damn phone?"

He shrugged, his tuxedo coat shifting under her cheek. "I've been getting these all day. It's around eight o'clock in the evening in California, so I imagine that they're getting frantic, trying to raise me before it's too late to call. Let me put that on airplane mode." He reached behind himself to grab it.

"Surely everybody in the law firm can't need references already."

"It's the clients."

"You aren't the one who was swindling them! They should be calling Val and Josie."

"They've been arrested, so they won't be answering their phones."

Rox grabbed her chest. "Oh my God!"

"As influential as the studios are, our clients have the weapon of public outrage on their side. The DA filed some interim charges while they investigate the matter. No, the clients want me back." He flipped off the flashlight mode and held up the screen so she could see the list of text messages in the deep darkness of the gazebo.

"Back?" She squinted at the phone, the screen too bright to stare at directly after the darkness of the night.

He nodded. "The studios want to renegotiate all the contracts, every single one of them, that passed through Val's or Josie's hands because there's a very good chance that an actor could go to court and have them declared fraudulent. Thus, the studios and recording companies may have distributed hundreds of movies and thousands of songs that they don't quite hold the rights to."

The gazebo spun around Rox, and she grabbed the bench. *"Oh, Lord."*

"The clients want me to start my own law firm. I've got a standard reply now that I'm pasting in that I cannot represent them in any action concerning Val and Josie due to conflict of interest. It's not ethical."

"And so they're backing off." Rox nodded and swiveled on the bench.

His phone buzzed in his hand again, and he stared at it. "It's making them froth at the mouth. They're insistent. Even though I have assured them that I cannot possibly represent them in the case against our previous firm, their attempts at bribery know no bounds."

"That doesn't sound like a bad thing."

"They want me to renegotiate their contracts with the studios and recording companies."

Rox turned to him. "And that's bad, why?"

"I'm not sure I'll be able to go back to California at all. Or if I do, my sister will send a regiment to look after me. She means well."

Rox tapped her chin with one finger. "So we could go home."

"The security would be oppressive. Rotating shifts. Chauffeured armored cars. It's really no way to live."

"How about if we lived someplace like New York?"

"Probably marginally less security. My sister is not taking these threats and attempts lightly."

"But the attacks were when those guys thought that you were just some anonymous entertainment-industry lawyer. They thought you didn't have the resources to defend yourself. Did Val or Josie ever know about your 'dynastic problems?'"

"I see you figured out what Arthur meant."

"Obviously. Did they?"

"I took great pains to make sure that no one knew. When I applied for the position at the firm, right out of law school, I asked my professors and other references to call them immediately. I had the transcripts sent over from Yale Law before they could ask. They did a criminal record check, but I don't have any problems with that. My credit rating was not a problem."

Yeah, Rox bet that his credit was absolutely sterling. "So Val and Josie never knew. Monty and his partners never knew. They thought you were just some lawyer. They will probably poop their pants when they find out. Oh, what I wouldn't give to be a fly on the wall when he sees you arrive with security commandos and snipers and a flippin' tank rolling through the middle of Los Angeles."

Casimir smiled. "It would certainly change the situation."

"Can you imagine? Monty would be sitting there in his office, at that long, stupid conference table of his, and the door blows open and a squad of black-fatigued, gun-toting commandos storm into the room, throw him on the table and frisk him, and then slam him back into his chair. Then we stroll in and tell him that we need to talk to him about certain clauses in his contracts."

He was chuckling now. "The look on his face would be priceless."

"And then if he starts stalling and telling us that we're crazy because we think the contract should be different, you lift one finger and all those commandos point their guns at him in one coordinated move, and then his water glass shatters because a sniper shot it from somewhere outside."

Casimir laid a hand on his stomach because he was laughing so hard. "I would almost feel sorry for him."

Rox gazed into the darkness, imagining something even worse. "And then after he signs the contracts, the windows would get blown out of the room, and we would go jump onto zip lines and be zipped up into a hovering black helicopter."

Casimir was past laughing now, his voice rising as he bent sideways and giggled. "Oh, my Lord. *Stop.* Please, *stop.*"

Rox snaked her arms around his waist and hugged him, even though he was still giggling helplessly, almost lying on the bench. "And that's just how we'll do it."

Chapter Eighty-Four

THE AMSBERG LAW FIRM

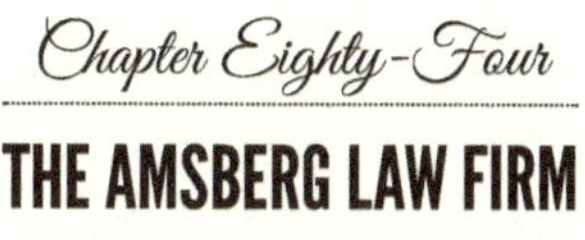

The ribbon-cutting ceremony was held inside a Los Angeles skyscraper, in the office of the new law firm that occupied the entire floor. Spring California sunlight flooded through the walls of glass on two sides of the lobby.

Rox had wanted the ribbon-cutting ceremony to be held outside in the spring air, but Lachlan and the other security people first counseled against it, then argued against it, and then out-right declared that it was not going to happen. Even though there had been no incidents since Casimir and Rox had returned to California, and even though dozens of arrests had been made once Val and Josie had started naming other people involved in the criminal scheme to defraud their clients, Ana and Casimir both erred on the side of caution whenever there might be an opportunity for an attack.

Especially since Rox had discovered that she was pregnant.

This happened, luckily, only a few days after the Dutch Parliament passed an Act of Consent to allow Casimir to marry her and still stay within the line of succession to the throne. Indeed, once the government had presented the bill to the parliament, it had passed within hours, surprising even Ana with how little debate it had taken. They hadn't even needed to hold a reception for the MPs to meet Rox.

It was as if keeping Casimir and his future, hypothetical children in the line of succession had been in everyone's best interest.

After they had gotten the parliament's approval and admitted that there might be an addition to the royal family rather sooner than expected, Ana had insisted on planning and holding the wedding within a month.

It was almost as if Ana had a vested interest in adding new members to the royal family and the line of succession as soon as possible, too.

Every time Crown Princess Ana saw Rox, she started the conversation by squealing and asking if she had felt anything yet, even though she must have known from her own four pregnancies that it was too early.

She kept slipping Rox baby clothes, too. Really nice ones.

And jewelry, insisting that Rox needed diamonds to wear at state events, even though Casimir had to be threatened and cajoled into accepting invitations. He was getting better about them, though. With

Rox by his side, that real smile reached his dark green eyes more often than before.

So, on that lovely spring California day, at the opening of their law firm, Casimir and Rox both held the oversize scissors and cut the orange and blue ribbon inside the lobby to officially open The Amsberg Law Office.

Rox had wanted to call the firm Amsberg and Amsberg, but Casimir had bitten his lip and explained law firm ethics: Under the Rules of Professional Responsibility, only attorneys who had been admitted to the bar could form a partnership and be included in the name of the law firm. Paralegals and other lawyers could be employed by a law firm, but paralegals could not have a financial interest in the firm.

After Rox had finished her temper tantrum, Casimir had explained that they would make sure in their pre-nup that she owned a fifty-percent stake in the corporation that would own the law firm.

And after she finished her temper tantrum about having a pre-nup at all, Casimir assured her that the half-interest in the law firm would be one of the few items in there, and other than that, all their assets would be considered community property.

Including the cats.

If they ever got divorced, Casimir wanted sole custody of Pirate.

After that temper tantrum that only ended when Rox threatened to go biblical on him, they agreed on shared custody of the cats.

And any children, they added.

They amended the agreement to stipulate shared custody of their *four* cats.

After their wedding in the Netherlands and honeymoon in Fiji, as Casimir had insisted, they had found a new house to live in while the mansion was being rebuilt into a security-bristling stronghold. During that time, Casimir had kept visiting the animal shelter with Rox, who was no longer allowed to clean the litter boxes and banished to doing admin work or walking the small and quiet dogs for the duration.

There, he continued to bond with Fairy Dust, the tiny cat who might have been feral but who loved him.

After a month, they brought her home.

Rox kept slipping Midnight extra shrimp treats to reward him for his loyalty.

At the reception at The Amsberg Law Office on that first official day of business, Rox rested for a few moments in her huge office before she went out to brave the crowd again. The couches in the meeting area were overstuffed, inviting people to stay and chat. The pillow-soft upholstery was heaven on her sore back.

She rested her hand on her growing, rounded tummy.

Only three more months.

A knock rattled the door on the side wall of her office.

Rox called, "Come in, honey."

Casimir stuck his head through the door that adjoined her office to his. The cheek with his two scars was toward her, now pale and healed, but quite noticeable. "Are you hiding in here?"

"Just admiring my new office."

Indeed, her new office had everything, the conversation grouping with couches and a coffee table, a huge desk worthy of the most distinguished barrister, and a bassinet and rocking chair in the corner.

He walked over to where she was sitting and sat beside her, plunking her feet in his lap to rub the sore spots on her insteps. She groaned and let her head flop back.

"They've broken out the champagne," he said.

"Two hours early. Should we send Wren for some more?"

"Last I saw her, she was dancing on a desk with a two-liter magnum of it in her hand."

"Lovely. Our staid and formal office opening has turned into an excuse for day-drinking."

He smiled. "With our staff, every office party will require a fleet of cabs to make sure everyone gets home safely."

Someone knocked on the door that led to the main office.

Rox glanced at the clock: straight up two in the afternoon. "Come in, Lachlan!"

He stuck his head in her office and glanced at them, appraised the room, and said, "Thank you, ma'am." He stepped back out and closed the door behind himself.

Casimir continued to massage her feet and ankles.

The security checks weren't oppressive, but they were constant.

"Come on," Casimir said, tickling the bottom of her foot. She jumped and pulled her feet out of his hands. "Let's go back for a few minutes. Must mingle with clients."

Rox allowed herself to be pulled to standing and wedged her swollen feet back into her flats. At least she had an excuse not to wear heels for a few more months.

Outside, in the office area, she sat with Melanie, Wren, and the rest of her lunch bunch ladies from the old law firm. Pretty much anyone who had wanted to come to the new law firm had been offered a position, which meant that work had gone on, almost without pause, ever since they had gotten back from the honeymoon.

It was just like how it should be, but with better security, a nicer office, Cash Amsberg in her bed every night, and no more snipers, firebombs, or manufactured car crashes.

She watched Casimir float through the crowd, greeting people and laughing, shaking hands and slapping backs.

In California, he really was everyone's friend and the life of the party, and now that he was thoroughly off the market, the women associates were actually treating him like a human being instead of a piece of ass.

He made his way closer to her, locking eyes from a few people away, but was intercepted by one of their clients who hadn't seen him for over a year, since her last contract for a romcom. She touched his cheek near the twisted scar tissue and pursed her plumped lips. "Good Lord, Cash. What happened to you there?"

Casimir grinned at the woman and glanced up at Rox. "It's a great story. Let me tell you about it."

Rox smiled at him and settled her hand on her tummy.

Countess Juliana kicked her palm.

Chapter Eighty-Five

A SPECIAL SNEAK PEEK OF: STIFF DRINK

Crows Fighting Over Crumbs

STIFF DRINK

ARTHUR

BLAIR BABYLON

Genevieve "Gen" Ward stood in the conference room of Serle's Court Barristers, a London law firm, eyeing dozens of manila folders strewn across the long table.

Her black, high-heeled shoes still bore traces of cold graveyard mud and shed dried flakes onto the rug, even though she had tried to wipe it off. Her cheeks felt starched-stiff from grinding her teeth during Horace Lindsey's funeral. Weeping at a funeral was so American. Horace would have been so disappointed in her if she had cried in front of all the other lawyers.

The folders on the table held the summaries of Horace's law cases that he had been fighting when he had died. Gen's future as a British trial lawyer, a barrister, rested on which of them she might be assigned.

Just not the case of Lord Arthur Finch-Hatten, the Earl

of Severn, she prayed to the capricious gods of the court. *Any case but that one.*

Outside the conference room's long windows, a fountain spouted water amid the formal garden's winter-dead lawns, as prim as any palace's grounds. The tall spires and walls of Lincoln's Inn—an antique, Gothic building that housed lawyers' business offices—surrounded the garden and blocked out the skyscrapers and honking cars of central London.

Inside the conference room, the sixty-odd other senior and junior barristers crowded around the table, craning their necks and shouldering each other for a better look at the labels typed on the folders' tabs.

Everyone was dressed in mourning black, and the gathered lawyers resembled vicious crows, ready to do battle over crumbs.

They would not, however, make a move toward the folders.

The Head Clerk, Celestia Alen-Buckley, stood at the head of the table, her short arms braced on the dark, carved wood as she glared at the folders strewn between the rows of hovering barristers.

The Head Clerk would decide who would be assigned to which case. Her dark eyes narrowed, watching the barristers, sizing each of them up even though she had known them all for decades. With just a glance, the lawyers shriveled under Celestia Alen-Buckley's gaze. Without her formidable power stretching over the table, the barristers might have leapt onto the table to melee for the cases, each worth many thousands of pounds and mostly completed.

All the black-clad lawyers and staff had just returned from the funeral of their esteemed, learned colleague Horace Lindsey, one of the most senior barristers in chambers. The kindly, grandfatherly man had taken a special interest in Gen. Her multiple disadvantages—having spent her formative years in America, retaining an abominable Texas accent despite her best efforts, her lack of the benefits of the British independent school education like most of her colleagues had enjoyed, and of course, her unfortunate appearance—had provoked his pity.

Her mother had assured Gen of her lack of looks her whole life, telling her that she had to be especially smart and diligent to make up for her long, horsey face and too-big teeth.

Her whole life.

Gen liked to think that she had grown into her face and teeth when she had stretched to a towering five feet and ten inches, but her mother had continued to harp on Gen's thick waist, her thunderous thighs, and her cankles.

So Gen worked like demon dog to make up for all her disadvantages.

Horace Lindsey had noticed Gen working late—all the other pupil barristers had left for the pubs and an evening of socializing and drinking—because Horace was still at his desk, too. They drank tea while they worked, and he had imparted the little bits of lore and advice that, as an outsider, she had sorely needed. Horace had thought of her as an up-and-comer, a grinder, despite all her disadvantages. He had been the first senior barrister to make a cup of tea for Gen, one late evening while they were listening to streaming music while they worked. She had practically fallen in love with him and his sparse, white hair when he had presented her with a hot cup of tea and a wry, wrinkled smile. He had become her pupil master for the first six months of her internship, called a pupillage.

Horace had suffered a heart attack at his desk just a few days before, late at night, a few weeks after Christmas. Gen had called the ambulance while he had clutched his chest, and then Gen had told Horace's partner, Basil, that his last words were of him.

They weren't, of course. Horace's last words had been instructions on his cases. Gen had taken notes with one hand and held Horace's meaty fist with the other while he gasped, suffocating. He had been desperate to leave those final instructions on his cases, and she had printed out every word and stapled them into the manila folders littered on the conference room table.

And now all the senior, junior, and pupil barristers in chambers hovered over Horace's folders, nudging each other as they peered at the labels, ready to pounce on the most prestigious cases or the ones most easily won or settled.

Genevieve was a lowly pupil barrister, the lowest

rung on the barrister ladder, still in her first six-month term of law practical training, only recently speaking for clients in court with Horace looking over her shoulder the whole time. The Head Clerk would assign her the dregs of Horace's cases to write the briefs for a new pupil master.

If she got any at all.

Just not Lord Severn's case, she prayed again.

Lord Arthur Finch-Hatten, the Earl of Severn, had been one of Horace's most difficult cases. His younger brother, John Finch-Hatten, was suing him for possession and control of the family's earldom and several estates. For any other defendant, this would have been designated a frivolous lawsuit that would have gotten the filing lawyer assigned costs or disciplined by the Bar Council.

Except that the defendant was The Right Honorable Arthur Finch-Hatten, the twenty-fifth Earl of Severn, the notorious and incorrigible scoundrel, *damn it.*

When Lord Severn deigned to grace the law offices with his presence to discuss the lawsuit against him, he strutted through chambers, the walking incarnation of privilege and sin. His deftly tailored suits were cut close to his muscular body as if he had been carved from dark marble. His strong cheekbones and square jaw were the pinnacles of centuries of beautiful women bred to powerful men to produce stunning gentlemen and ladies in the next generations. His ancestral tree was studded with several kings of England and Scotland, several more and farther back than the current heir to the British throne could claim.

As Lord Severn strode through the chambers, his silvery-blue eyes roamed, surveying the female admins and junior barristers, deciding which of them to tempt into a night or a week of exorbitant debauchery. Dark hair fell across his forehead, and the subtle scent of some hideously expensive cologne —warm spices and clean musk—wafted from him as he passed Gen, who always seemed to be caught out of her tiny office when he arrived. She would rather have barred her door against his influence.

Lord Severn usually left the barristers' chambers with a young woman hanging on his arm and smiling up at his arrogant face, and then Horace had scoured the gossip websites with trepidation until the woman came back to work, shame-faced but oddly exuberant and dripping with new jewelry. His superficial relationships never lasted longer than a few weeks.

Lord Severn was a silver-eyed, silver-spoon-fed, silver-tongued billionaire, which was absolutely everything they needed him *not* to be.

Gen prayed that she would not have to deal with Horace's most problematic case.

The tan file folders splayed across the table.

Gen waited quietly, her hands clasped in front of her.

The other barristers did the same.

Celestia Alen-Buckley examined each file and made her pronouncements.

Some folders, she perused the stickers and pursed her lips, deliberating, her eyes picking out a few barristers as possibilities, before she handed them off.

Some folders only received a cursory glance and a deliberate throw to a senior barrister.

Evidently, some considerations had already been made behind the scenes.

Damn it. Gen should have lobbied to be assigned the Lombardi case. With Horace's wise and gentle instructions, it should settle soon. Gen needed a few wins in her docket.

She needed court wins *a lot.*

Tenancy offers—an invitation to set up shop as a "tenant" within the chambers, essentially a job offer to be a litigating lawyer in the law firm—would be made nine months from then, at the end of September. If the senior barristers didn't offer tenancy to Gen, it would destroy her career just as it had officially begun. No other chambers would take her on. She would have few options to salvage her career, and they were all bad.

Gen's new boss, Octavia Hawkes, stood across the table from Gen, eyeing the manila folders littering the dark wood table. Octavia's blond hair was tightly coiffed into a French twist, as it always was on court days. Her black suit clung to her slender body. Her tailor came to her home once a month to adjust any suit that wasn't a perfect fit.

Yep, glamorous, successful Octavia Hawkes was

Gen's new boss and her competition for Horace's best cases.

Gen needed to snag *several* of those cases or at least one really good one.

Most pupil barristers were in debt, of course, unless they had wealthy parents who had ponied up the cash for their education. Gen sure as heck hadn't had that advantage, either. The bar course had cost thirty thousand pounds for the year-long session. Thirty thousand pounds of debt, and Gen owed that money to her mother.

And her mother needed it back *now.*

Not in five years. Certainly not in ten.

Right *now.*

Celestia Alen-Buckley divvied up the cases.

The Lombardi folder whisked across the table to James Knightly, one of the other first-sixers who was vying for a tenancy offer. James had brought a caramel macchiato to the funeral and handed it to Celestia Alen-Buckley, and now James had the Lombardi file.

James played the barrister game exceptionally well. His father was a judge.

Gen mentally kicked herself again for not cozying up to the Celestia Alen-Buckley yesterday and this morning. She ought to have known better.

File by file, Celestia Alen-Buckley made her pronouncements, her dusky hands flipping the folders across the table to be grabbed by their intended recipients too fast for Gen to keep track of them.

Finally, only one folder remained on the table.

Please, not Arthur Finch-Hatten. Please, God. Not Arthur Finch-Hatten.

Celestia Alen-Buckley picked up that last folder and looked straight at her.

Gen tried not to shrink under the woman's stare.

Celestia Alen-Buckley whipped the folder down the long tabletop, the paper whispering on the wood the whole way. It skidded to a stop right where Gen stood.

"Here, Genevieve," Celestia said. "You're ambitious. If you can win it, you'll make your name here."

Gen was reaching for the folder when she saw the label, a blur of black ink on white with three capital letters sticking up: an *A,* an *F,* and an *H.*

Damn it.

FIRST MEETING

Gen's first meeting with her new client, the scandalous Lord Arthur Finch-Hatten, the Earl of Severn, was scheduled for eleven o'clock the next morning.

Her handwritten notes covered the inside of his manila folder:

Call him Lord Severn, My Lord, or Your Lordship. Not Mr. Finch-Hatten. Certainly not Arthur or Hey Hottie Sugar-Buns.

Don't offer to shake his hand. You're a barrister for God's sake, and barristers don't do that.

Don't stare at him. Act like a damn professional.

The meeting was not to be held in her cubby of an office at Serle's Court Barristers. In her office, her pupil desk was hardly larger than her laptop and couldn't have held even a fraction of the documents that she needed to go over with him.

Instead, Gen had reserved the smallest of the conference rooms for the all-important first meeting.

The windows looked outward from the building over the winding streets of central London, lined closely with brick structures like a medieval city. The other side, the *good* side of the building, faced the courtyard garden.

In the conference room, the heavily carved table seemed ridiculously ornate to Gen, but she had grown up in America. Her bourgeois tastes ran more to clean lines and modern furniture rather than the trappings of wealth and history that were the norm in British barristers' chambers. She needed to get used to this kind of thing.

She waited in the conference room for Lord Severn to show up.

By eleven in the morning, Gen had made good progress on her work for the day and had drunk several all-important cups of coffee.

That morning, she had also prepared several more cups of coffee for her new pupil mistress, Octavia Hawkes, who took her coffee at a piping-hot one hundred eighty degrees Fahrenheit, which is eighty-two centigrade after Gen converted it in her head from the American stuff to the British thing. Octavia also required exactly one quarter cup of half-and-half that Gen purchased twice-weekly from the market on her way to work and no sugar. Gen made Octavia's coffee perfectly five times per office day, or else Octavia's crimson-painted lips retracted into a red dot of anger on her face.

Gen didn't want to see the red dot of anger.

Every time it appeared, Gen's chances to obtain tenancy in the law chambers dropped a little.

Pupil barristers always made and served coffee for their pupil masters or mistresses. Gen had made Horace's tea during her first six, though after the first month, they had been making tea for each other.

The student lawyers also wheeled in the silver tea service and chocolate cookies at high tea every day at four-thirty, and they served the drinks at the chambers' occasional cocktail parties. It was a very British way of putting baby barristers in their place: making them serve their betters like actual servants.

But that morning, Gen waited in the conference room, fiddling with a pen, shuffling the stacks of papers associated with the Finch-Hatten case, and drinking her third cup of coffee. The cookies over on the sideboard called to her, even though they were the plain biscuits that they served to clients, not the chocolate ones that the barristers reserved for themselves at tea.

Lord Severn was late.

The lazy libertine had struck again. He had probably been out carousing and womanizing until the wee hours of the morning, perhaps a belated New Year's party, and had only just gotten his privileged arse out of bed. When Horace Lindsey had arranged meetings with Lord Severn, Horace had joked that he always set the meeting for half past the hour in his own schedule, but he had told the rascal

Lord Severn to be at the offices on the hour and started charging him then.

She did her best not to grind her teeth. It was all billable hours, after all. Lord Severn was paying her to wait for him.

But twenty-five minutes was excessive.

Gen's pupil mistress, Octavia Hawkes, would have said, "Tardiness robs us of opportunity and the dispatch of our forces," one of her quotes from Machiavelli. Octavia liked *The Prince* and Sun Tzu's *The Art of War* a little too much.

As she had control over Gen's entire future, Gen studied both books so she could hold a coherent conversation with Octavia.

Horace Lindsey had preferred Shakespeare, and his quotes were still marked on some of his clients' file folders.

Like all lawyers who were waiting for a scheduled meeting, Gen busied herself with yet another case and billed that client for her time, too. Racking up the billable hours was another way to distinguish herself from the other pupil barristers who were competing for a tenancy offer.

Of course, everyone was doing that.

Gen needed to do something *smart,* something *exceptional.*

Something besides waiting for Lord Severn to show himself.

Even Horace's death from overwork hadn't shamed the irascible Lord Severn into mending his ways.

Gen straightened the stacks of papers on the table. She had read over and taken notes on all of them over the last few days, even though it should have been an easily winnable case.

Honestly, the Finch-Hatten case should never come to trial. No solicitor nor barrister should have touched the complaint.

Lord Severn's parents had died in a car accident when he and his younger brother had been small children. As was customary, they had not divided the earldom and properties but had left the vast majority of the estates to the eldest son, Arthur. They had bequeathed only enough money for an excellent education and a nest egg to his younger brother, John. Preserving the great estates in this manner was still common practice.

There had been no way for Arthur's parents to know that Arthur would become a lascivious wastrel, while his brother, John, would become an upstanding doctor with ties to Doctors Without Borders and do *pro bono* work in the most disadvantaged parts of London.

But even if they had known how their two sons would turn out, it probably wouldn't have made a difference.

After their parents' deaths, the younger brother, John, had gone to Eton and other very British independent schools to prepare him for an excellent career because he would have to work for a living.

Arthur Finch-Hatten had been raised in one of the world's most expensive boarding schools in

Switzerland, *Institut Le Rosey*, where the very wealthy dumped their inconvenient children.

No wonder the poor sod had turned out so badly, Gen mused. He hadn't stood a chance. Everyone at that hoity-toity school probably had the work ethic of a sloth with a Quaalude problem.

Arthur had grown up among the offspring of Saudi sheiks, deposed European royalty, African and Latin American dictators, politicians and business-people from every continent, and Russian mobsters. The joke was that Le Rosey held their parent-teacher conferences in conjunction with the World Economic Forum that took place in January in Davos, Switzerland because many of the parents were in town that week, anyway. "Davos" is the annual event where the world's twenty-five hundred most powerful people gather to discuss their world domination and to ski. Some of the world's most effective security forces, supplemented by elite mercenaries, kept back the conspiracy theorists and anarchists who protested outside and at a considerable distance.

Her phone screen read eleven-thirty.

Gen shuffled the papers, checking over her notes.

Maybe, like Horace, she should have just assumed that Lord Severn would be at least half an hour late and scheduled other clients' appointments in the meantime.

She whiled away the hour, her professional meter ticking off her ever-increasing fee, staring at the pages of the brief in her hand and wondering why the case had even gotten this far. It seemed that any judge should have thrown this out.

The parents had written their will.

It was a legal will.

It was aligned with the laws and customs of England.

The estate had been settled twenty years before.

Gen didn't see how John could even contest it.

Except that the defendant was the notorious rake, Lord Severn.

She was still staring at the paper when Miriam, one of the junior clerks, opened the conference room door and leaned inside, giggling. "Your client is here," she practically sprayed.

Miriam never *sprayed* anything. The clerk was the soul of decorum and took care of Gen's fees with the utmost professionalism.

Miriam withdrew, and the door gaped wider.

Gen steeled herself for battle. This client who was a walking waste of oxygen wasn't going to put one over on her.

Lord Severn strolled into the room, his long legs covering the carpet at a quick pace even though he walked leisurely.

Gen had seen Lord Severn before, of course, but she had dodged behind other people and scurried back to her office while he had met with Horace. A nobleman with such an outrageous fee always commanded the attention of the most senior barrister in the office.

When he strolled in, Lord Arthur Finch-Hatton, the Earl of Severn, was still staring straight ahead at the window that overlooked the crowded streets of central London, so Gen's first look at him was his profile.

Morning sunlight streaming in the window clung to his golden skin. His cheekbones were hard slashes, and his jaw was a sharp right angle above the crisp, white collar of the dress shirt and black business suit he wore. His lush lips curved in a smile, as if looking over London from such a prestigious advantage suited him. The subtle lift of his chin and roll of his broad shoulders suggested that, had history been different, he might have ruled the land that spread beneath the window.

He turned to survey the rest of the room and caught Gen sitting at the table, gaping at him.

Oh, God. She was *staring.*

He always caught her staring.

She was staring at the black curls of his dark hair that stroked his ears and the back of his neck, and she was staring at the way his very precisely tailored suit skimmed his strong shoulders and the rounded biceps of his arms and then narrowed at his waist and hips, and she was staring at his extravagant height and his long legs and the way his head tilted with amusement as he caught her staring at him *again.*

Gen's brain turned to goo.

Damn, Lord Severn was one gorgeous man.

No, no, no.

No, Gen was a highly trained barrister, not a silly schoolgirl meeting a good-looking man for the first time. She had seen lots of handsome men.

Lots of them.

Lots.

Lots-lots-lots-lots-lots. The goo in her mind grew fuzzy tendrils, and cotton candy filled her skull and stopped up her ears.

Her thoughts slowed as she met his eyes.

My God. His *eyes.*

His eyes weren't blue or gray or any color that she had ever seen on a real human being before.

His eyes shimmered with an unexpected delight and intelligence.

They narrowed when he smiled that good-natured, natural smile that beckoned to her.

And most of all, his eyes sparkled *silver* and were bounded by a dark blue ring.

They were beguiling, magical, unearthly.

That was not damn *fair.*

Gen had heard about peoples' knees weakening, but she was already sitting down. Still, her bones turned to soft clay, and she grabbed the sides of her chair because she was in danger of slithering out of it and onto the carpeting under the conference room table.

Lord Severn walked toward her.

It was customary for barristers to stand when greeting a client.

She should stand up. *You really should stand up.*

Stand up, dammit.

Gen gripped sides of the chair and pushed with her arms to lift herself to her feet.

Even though too-tall Gen was wearing blunt, two-inch heels, Lord Severn was still *inches* taller than she was. At least four inches. Which meant he was at least six-four.

Blathering. Her brain was *blathering.*

His tie was the same azure-silver as his eyes but glimmering silk.

Goddamn it. She had seen Lord Severn before, *several times,* and he *always* had this effect on her.

Her and pretty much *every* person who was sexually attracted to men. One of the clerks, Roland, had actually fainted after Lord Severn had left chambers one time.

She should have gotten immune to him with subsequent exposures, *right?* This crazy reaction should have worn off by now, *right?*

Dizziness spun her head, and she gasped for air because she had forgotten how to *breathe.*

At her stupid sucking sound, Lord Severn smiled, though it was a sad smile like he regretted that his mere presence was overwhelming her so.

He pulled out a chair on the other side of the table. "I was terribly sorry to hear about Horace Lindsey's untimely death. He was an excellent barrister and a family friend."

Even though it was only eleven-thirty in the morning, Lord Severn's breath carried a faint whiff of whiskey under the mint, like he had just come from a gentleman's brunch.

Gen's mind searched for words.

Any words.

Wut arrre werdz.

She gathered her brain together and squeezed something out.

"Yes, it was a great loss to us all," she managed.

Lord Severn nodded. "He spoke highly of you. I'm pleased that you will be taking over my case."

"You *are?*" she blurted. Oh, good grief. Could she be any more junior-high school? "I mean, Mr. Lindsey did a great deal of work preparing for this case. I'm honored to argue it in his stead."

"Horace and I always discussed my case over a liquid lunch at my club. Why don't you skive off work for a few hours and enjoy my hospitality?"

"Oh, I couldn't," Gen said. "I'm due in court with Ms. Hawkes this afternoon."

"When?"

"Three o'clock."

"I could have you back by then."

"But I have to read the briefs that the solicitors sent over so that I know what I'm arguing." Her native Texas accent broadened in her mouth. "What use is a hired gun if they don't know whom to shoot?"

Lord Severn tilted his head. The corner of his lips twitched up. "Horace didn't mention that you were American."

Damn. Gen had been living in London for several years. Surely, most of her American accent should have faded away. She was trying like the Devil to enunciate, but evidently, she was still garbling her marbles. "I was raised in the States until I was seventeen, when my mother and I moved back London."

"So you're a British citizen?"

None of Gen's other clients had worried about what color passport she presented at customs. "Yes, I was born here. I have American citizenship, too, because when I was a kid in Texas, my dad made sure of it. I still travel with my US passport sometimes."

Lord Severn leaned on his elbows on the table and watched her. "And why would you use an American passport when you travel?"

The laser-like focus of his silvery eyes blinded her, and Jesus, he had *dimples* when he smiled.

Gen stuttered, "Masochism?"

Lord Severn laughed and adjusted his tie. The silver silk flashed in the sunlight, and his eyes took on a metallic sheen. "There's something you won't hear a barrister admit to every day."

"Yes, well, barristers don't admit to a lot of things."

"Do tell." His voice was warm with amusement as if he liked her.

"Oh, I couldn't say. Professional courtesy."

"Said the bishop to the actress."

"Quite." She laughed at him. Her laugh didn't sound like a nervous cackle, either, which was a small miracle.

"I can only imagine what those other barristers do," he said, and his eyes *twinkled.*

Jesus, Lord. How did he get his eyes to *twinkle* like that? They practically *glittered* with white-hot sparks, and Gen felt herself leaning forward and swaying her back like a broken-down mare to push out her boobs, two of her few decent physical assets. She admitted, "Sometimes, we play games in court."

"What kinds of games?" he asked.

Go ahead, his voice implied. *Say something outrageous, something unprofessional, something sexy.*

Gen giggled. "One judge plays online poker all day while hearing cases, so we find him online and take his money while we're arguing the cases."

Lord Severn's jaw dropped a little. "Does he know that you're playing against him?"

"Oh, heavens, no. But if you win the case and the money from him, then the losing barrister has to buy a round for the pub that night."

Lord Severn leaned in. "Are there any others?"

Gen whispered, "Like, we give each other a list of words that we have to work in during arguments."

He asked, "What kinds of words?"

In his high-bred, arch English accent, his open-ended question couldn't have sounded dirty, and yet there was just the suggestion that, if she said something naughty, he would be even more amused.

"Anything. Last time, the words were encumbered, rectitude, and nabob."

"Oh, you barristers and your vocabulary. Horace said that he admired your wit."

"He did not," Gen said.

"Oh, yes. He was quite taken with you, in his own way, of course."

"Of course."

"He thought that you would make an excellent QC or a judge."

Gen blinked, trying to process that Horace thought she could rise so high. "That's more than I could hope for."

"And yet he saw it in you." Lord Severn leaned back in his chair and crossed one leg over the other.

His pant leg rode up above his ankle.

The precisely tailored suit that he wore was soft black, as were his shoes, but his socks were *teal.*

Shockingly *teal.*

His ankles were a flash of Caribbean-sea color in the very conservative English barristers' chambers.

Nothing that Gen was wearing had anywhere near that kind of color. Her pale gray blouse, black suit, pearl earrings, and beige-toned stockings and underwear were all respectable.

It wasn't every day that someone wore teal socks into a trial lawyer's office. Most clients were in a battle for their lives. They might lose or win a great deal of money or be sent to jail at the end of their trials. Most people wore their somber, Sunday best into her office to discuss the strategy and their odds.

The vibrant color of Lord Severn's teal sock was so unexpected, so *careless,* that Gen felt like a Victorian matron offended by a glimpse of a table leg that should have been covered by a modest lace skirt.

Oh, Lord. She was staring at his ankle, a trim ankle that led up his leg to a swell of calf muscle.

She had to stop.

Stop looking.

Gen snapped her eyes up to his face.

Lord Severn's smile grew. "Something amusing?"

"No." She pointedly did not look near his foot.

He did, however. "My socks amuse you?"

"No."

"A barrister wouldn't wear anything so whimsical, would they?"

"Of course not. A judge might actually take offense, thinking that the barrister was flaunting the dignity of the court."

Lord Severn said, "Because you're in the professions. A man matches his socks to his pants. A gentleman matches his socks to his mood."

Gen steeled herself not to ask how he chose his underwear. "I can't imagine what sort of mood you're in to choose such an—" she didn't look down at them, "—unusual color."

"I'm a creature of many appetites, it's true." Though he was still smiling, his gaze didn't waver from her eyes as he said this.

And right there, with Lord Severn's words and his sultry glance that turned his silver eyes molten, their conversation went from casual banter, a pointless conversation that meant nothing to either of them, to something heated and with the suggestion of an offer, a implied extension of his hand to go wherever he might lead her.

Gen stared down at the paperwork she was holding, trying to steady her hands. "We need to go over this information," she said. Her voice sounded thin in her own ears. "Is this contact information correct?"

He took the paper from her outstretched fingers, and she snatched her hand back as if his touch might burn her.

He held the paper pinched in his fingers as he scanned the list. "This next-of-kin bit is John's information, my brother who is suing me. Quite honestly, we weren't raised on the same continent. The last time I saw him for any length of time, he was seven, and I was ten years old."

"Are you estranged?" she asked, unsure how to put that politely.

Lord Severn laughed. "Estranged doesn't begin to cover it. Let me add a few contact numbers." He snagged one of the several pens rolling across the conference room table and wrote in neat block letters in the margin of the paper. "If I'm ever in trouble or in hospital, call these two: Casimir van Amsberg and Maxence Grimaldi. These are their private numbers. Max is often out of cell phone range. Leave a message for him. It will take both a while to get to England, so plan for that. If I die, and *only* if I die, call this last number, too."

"Oh, I'm sure *that* won't happen." She paused. "You aren't sick or anything, are you?"

"Healthy as can be. I plan to die in my own bed of advanced old age, preferably by being stepped on by an elephant." He cleared his throat, as if he usually added something else to that sentence but hadn't.

"An elephant? In your bedroom?" she asked.

"It's as likely as anything else."

Gen glanced at the paper and read upside down. "Elizabeth? No last name?"

"Yes, ask for Elizabeth, and then tell them what happened to me and answer any questions they have with all the information you know."

"Is she your family solicitor? Or the estate's?"

"I'd better write them down, too." He did. "This is the number for my groundskeeper at Spencer House. He could handle the day-to-day functioning until the estate is settled."

That seemed like a lot of information for just a barrister to have. "Are you sure you're not planning to die?" she asked.

He looked up at her, grinning. "No one plans to die, and yet so few people truly *live.*"

"I'm sure most people live for quite some time."

Lord Severn laughed, a ringing, joyful sound. "Not like me. Every day, every single day, I *live.*"

Yes, and they needed to talk about how he *lived,* too.

"Now," he said, leaning in, "let's talk about getting you out of this cubicle and onto my plane to the continent tonight. I know a guy who thinks he's a rock star. Perhaps we can see his show from backstage and disabuse him of the notion, afterward."

Partying with rock stars was absolutely part of the problem. "Mr. Finch-Hatten—"

"Lord Severn," he said.

Gen glanced behind her, looking to see if someone was standing there.

"No, *I'm* Lord Severn," he said. "I'm a third-rank peer of the realm. One uses 'Lord' and my title as the Earl of Severn. I sign letters and documents as Severn, rarely with my surname."

"I'm sorry." Her hands fluttered over the paper in front of her, where she had written that note *right there* to call him that.

"It's perfectly all right, just something you should know."

"I'm *so* sorry. I hope you aren't offended." She grabbed the table to keep her hands from flopping off like brain-damaged bats.

"No offense taken," *Lord Severn* said. His hand lifted and hovered across the table, gently falling toward where her hands were braced against the dark wood.

Gen pushed back from the table, scooting the chair across the thick carpeting. "I think we should begin to discuss your case by going over some of the depositions. I have transcripts. The transcripts are right behind me, in the files. I'll just get one of the transcripts so we can discuss your case."

She bolted out of her chair and scrambled for

the table, pretending to sort through a file folder while she fought herself.

Her hands tingled. She shook them, flicking her fingers to try to fling the crazies away.

Spidery nerves crawled up her arms.

Not now, not now. She knew Lord Severn hadn't meant anything by their conversation and certainly not about being *a creature with appetites.* A little harmless flirting never killed anyone.

He wasn't flirting with her anyway. No one flirted with horsey-face Gen unless they wanted something, or it was a dare, or they were a predator with a taste for the weak and stupid.

Deep breath, deep breath.

Her skin stilled, and her body quieted. The panic drained away, a small blip in her day that would have no effect on the afternoon or the rest of this meeting, she resolved.

Time to get back to work.

Gen walked her fingers through the tabs sticking out of the block of files in the box. "It's in here somewhere. Do you want me to ring up the clerks and have some coffee or tea delivered?"

She *felt* him standing at her back rather than having heard him move.

The skin on the back of her neck heated, and a smoky shadow loomed up the white wall in front of her like an evil poltergeist trying to break through the centuries-old plaster.

His voice, whispering near her shoulder as he bent down, was low in his throat. "Or we could go back to my apartment for a liquid lunch. Or perhaps to Majorca for the weekend, to become better acquainted as barrister and client."

He trailed his fingers over the outside of her upper arm, the merest suggestion of a caress.

Training kicked in.

Gen jabbed with her elbow, striking backward as hard as she could.

Her blow was deflected sideways before she connected with his solar plexus.

She spun and kicked.

Air. No contact.

She flipped around as her kick whiffed through the air and stumbled backward, banging her hip on the table.

Lord Severn stood several paces behind her, angled sideways, his arms up and ready to block again. His hands were balled into loose fists so he could either strike or block. His steady gaze was serious over his fists.

He said, "I'm sorry. I misunderstood our banter, earlier."

"Don't touch me," she said, and the crazy shaking filled her hands and spread up her arms. "Don't *ever* touch me."

His voice was solemn. "As I said, I misunderstood. I won't approach you again." It sounded like a promise. "Are you all right?"

Gen leaned against the table with the boxes of file folders. The air felt chunky in her throat as she tried to breathe it, choking her. "I don't like that sort of thing."

"As I said, my mistake. I didn't mean to cause offense, and I won't presume again. I apologize for my error."

She was still breathing too fast in panicky gasps. *Damn.* Krav Maga lessons for two years, and she hadn't landed a blow when it had mattered. "I'll bet you're not used to women telling you no."

"I'm not used to misreading signals." Lord Severn lowered his hands, though he kept them near his waist and in front of him.

She had gotten caught up in the moment. She should have shut down any sort of invitation, fast. Her heart pounded in her chest, vibrating down her weak legs.

"I'm not used to men hitting on me," Gen admitted.

"Why not?"

She stared at him, at that gorgeous man with his testosterone-molded cheekbones and geometric jaw and those silvery eyes lined with dark lashes. He had probably never felt like the fat, ugly, lumbering giant in the corner of a party where everyone else was a pretty little elf. *"Look at me."*

Lord Severn blinked and lowered his hands to his sides. "You're funny and smart and attractive. Horace doted on you. He said once that he would adopt you if he thought you would stand for it, which was his highest praise. I quite imagine that men are all over you."

A laugh caught in her throat and turned into a snort.

Oh, that was sophisticated. Way to complete the image of the horsey, designated fat friend. She didn't even have her pretty girlfriends around to make her seem like the good-natured buddy.

She tried to cover up the snort by saying, "Uh, no. The men are *not* all over me."

And the thought of men being *all over her* made her legs shake.

Lord Severn said, "Their loss, then."

She tried to breathe more slowly, holding her breath between inhales, but fear still drowned her. "You probably only date beautiful duchesses and models and actresses and stuff."

He chuckled and took another step backward, putting more blessed space and air between them. "I've dated a few daft beauties. I had to measure every word I said lest they tattle to everyone they knew from lack of common sense. Handling women as if I'm manipulating a toddler to behave in public is tiresome."

Gen shook her hands to flick the heebie-jeebies out. She still wanted to scamper up the wall and cling to the ornate crown molding, shrieking curses down like a rabid spider monkey until Lord Severn left. "That sounds difficult."

Lord Severn walked around the table and sat in his chair. He gestured to the papers spread over the table. "Can we resume our discussion of my case?"

Gen nodded and drew a deep breath. She didn't

like saying this. She felt like a wuss. "I just need to find that deposition. Could you remain seated while I turn my back, if you would be so kind?"

Lord Severn patted the arm of his chair. "I won't move."

She gathered every ounce of her willpower and pivoted, turning her back to him, and started walking her fingers through the files. "I can call for coffee or tea."

"I would appreciate a coffee." His voice came from across the room and on the other side of the table.

Good.

The air around her seemed to thin, and Gen breathed more easily.

The papers under her fingers drifted into focus, and though she listened for any scuff of his chair moving or his tread on the thick carpeting, she only heard Lord Severn clear his throat a few times and rustle some papers, all on the far side of the table.

When she turned around, clutching the depositions, Lord Severn was leaning back in his chair, studying a piece of paper, entirely at ease.

He smiled at her. "Did you find the deposition?"

She nodded. Her neck felt stiff, like she was holding herself ready for him to assault her.

Gen dropped the papers on the table, letting the *swoosh* cover up her deep breath. She shook out her hands again.

"Okay, so let's talk about winning your case for you." She tapped the pile of papers in front of her with her pen, covering up that she was still flicking her fingers. "There's no mention of a jury strategy. It seems that Horace was preparing your case for an appeals court or magistrate instead of a trial."

Lord Severn shook his head. "Oh, no, no. We won't be going before a court at all. Matters of peerage are always heard in the House of Lords."

Gen grabbed papers, trying not to look like she was reading frantically. "Did Horace *say* that?"

"We discussed the case rather than the venue, but I assumed."

"Nothing is tried in the House of Lords anymore. Not since the Supreme Court was created in 2009. The last trial of a peer in the House was in 1935."

"But this is a matter of peerage, not a criminal case to be tried in the special court for nobles. The House of Lords always hears cases concerning peerage claims."

"But they never try cases anymore. They disbanded their court years ago. I think it was in 1948. The Law Lords aren't even members of the House of Lords anymore."

"But Horace said that we should appeal directly to the sovereign to throw it to the Lords."

Yes, yes. Gen could just remember from her university days that the Crown was the fount of all honor, and thus the Crown was entitled to decide all questions related to peerage disputes.

In practice, the sovereign referred all disputes about who got to be the duke to a committee in the

House of Lords—Gen wracked her brain—the Committee for Privileges and Conduct, and then the committee told the sovereign what to do in the case.

But the committee didn't even have Law Lords anymore, not since 2009. Surely, a bunch of stuffed shirts who weren't even barristers or solicitors couldn't decide such a contentious case based on law and precedent and honor without even Law Lords to advise them.

"Are you a member of the House of Lords?" she asked Lord Arthur Finch-Hatten, the Earl of Severn, just in case.

"Egads, no. My grandfather held his hereditary spot until the reform in 1999, but neither he nor I ever stood for election. I'm far too busy with other priorities."

Yeah, she just bet he was.

"I need to look over these depositions," Gen said, trying to come up with something to say that would not let on that she was entirely out of her depth.

"Quite," Lord Severn said drily and stood.

Oh, yeah. He knew.

"I just have to study this." She clutched the papers to keep her hands from shaking. "Give me a few days, and we'll meet again to discuss your case."

He brushed some non-existent lint from his suit jacket. "I'll find some way to occupy my time."

"No, you mustn't." Gen stood and let the papers in her hands flutter to the table. "Horace told me about your escapades. Every time you went on a bender, he watched the gossip sites for days, fretting that you might have given your brother yet more ammunition. The only reason this case has gotten this far is because of your atrocious behavior. For anyone else, anyone who acted with an ounce of decorum, such a stupid claim would have been dismissed immediately."

Lord Severn flicked his fingers in the air. "My actions don't matter. This is all a matter of peerage and privilege. My parents bequeathed the earldom and Spencer House to me."

"Your brother is getting the National Trust involved. Horace thought you might lose when he was fighting this for you."

"And now *you're* fighting it for me, so you see to it that my 'escapades' don't influence the case."

"Ms. Hawkes and I can't win your case if you're doing everything you can to sink it!"

Lord Severn sighed and looked out the window. "Be careful about that fiery American temper. The House of Lords won't like that."

"Nothing is ever tried in the House of *Lords!"*

His sultry glance down at her was laced with pity and derision, and Gen felt like a lower-class biscuit aping her betters.

Class will out, she had heard more than once when certain other pupil barristers had made unfortunate choices in alcohol quantities or sleeping arrangements. They had lost the respect of the senior barristers in chambers, and thus their chances at tenancy, with a single miscalculation.

But Lord Severn's disparaging stare made her feel all sorts of new levels of inferiority.

When he spoke, his cut-glass, upper-crust British accent clipped the words, "You need to do your homework."

Lord Severn turned on his heel and strode out of the room, his long legs covering the plush carpet in just a few steps.

Gen sank into her chair, holding her head in her hands.

Between her panicked freak-out and lack of understanding about Lord Severn's case, this meeting could not have gone any worse.

The only things worse than throwing the case to someone else was getting fired by the client or losing it in court.

And she had just increased the odds of both of those.

Disaster.

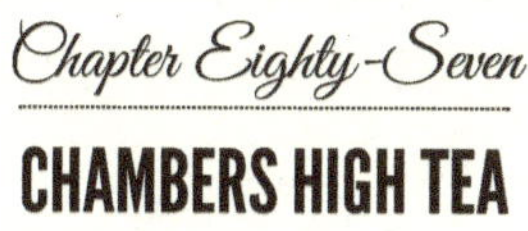

Chapter Eighty-Seven

CHAMBERS HIGH TEA

Chambers high tea was held at precisely four-thirty every day in the largest conference room. Pupil barristers brewed the tea in the enormous, Victorian-era silver tea set and served it in bone china cups to the barristers like waiters.

Outside the windows, the sun was already setting on the other side of the historic building that housed Lincoln's Inn, the wan winter sunlight barely able to crest over the roof and chimneys.

Gen poured a cup of tea for her boss, Octavia Hawkes, and added one lump of sugar, and then she poured another cup for one of the other senior barristers, David Trent, and another and another. The tea steamed sweetly, misting her cheeks with warmth and soft scent.

Beside her, fellow pupil barrister James Knightly poured tea for his pupil master, Leonard Boxster, and placed two of the chocolate cookies on the saucer for him. James blew across the top of the tea because Leonard Boxster liked his tea scandalously lukewarm. James said, "So I heard that you were *closeted* with His Lordship Arthur Severn this morning."

Gen grimaced at James's innuendo and poured tea for another senior barrister. "We had our first meeting to discuss his case."

James asked, "What's he like?"

Oh, that was a minefield. She couldn't say that Lord Severn was as hot as a blue brushfire in the Texas August sun, nor that he was funny, infuriating, and smelled like masculine devilry. "He's concerned about his case."

"That's not what I've heard."

"Then you've heard wrong. Of course, he's concerned about it. Who wouldn't be?"

"Someone who's too busy whoring and drinking his way across Europe."

Gen had left herself open for that one. "He met with me for a suitable amount of time, and we discussed his case. There was no whoring or drinking involved."

"How's he paying you? In cash or services rendered?"

What a smug ass. "His account was set up with the clerks when Horace Lindsey was his barrister."

"Must have been in services rendered, then."

Gen didn't bother scolding him. James had always been an arrogant, slimy asshole. Everything that came out of his mouth was a put-down or an outright lie. He was going to be an amazing barrister, and he was Gen's primary competition to get the one tenancy position at the law firm of Serle's Court Barristers.

She said, "Horace had better taste than Arthur Finch-Hatten."

James laughed and walked away, having gotten her to say something derogatory about a man who was better-looking and richer than he was.

And nicer.

Gen finally poured herself a cup of tea and sipped it.

Just a few more hours of work after tea time, and maybe she could go home for the day.

Unless the internet caught Arthur Finch-Hatten whoring and drinking his way across Europe again.

Chapter Eighty-Eight

ARTHUR'S DARK MISTRESS

STIFF DRINK

ARTHUR

3

BLAIR BABYLON

Arthur and Elizabeth had walked out into the deer park behind Spencer House. Though it was January, the mild afternoon was cool on his face, and the air drifted through the thick sweater he wore.

Elizabeth—no last name given, and her first name was not Elizabeth—appeared to be in her late forties, judging from the broad streaks of silver that ran from her temples to the blond French twist on the back of her head and the beginning of softness around her chin. Arthur didn't trust his approximation of her age, amongst other things.

The formal gardens checker-boarded the earth behind them, but out there in the deer park, wild grasses and trees grew in thickets of dense brush. In the distance, over by a copse of trees, a herd of over a hundred deer gamboled and grazed in the late afternoon sunlight. The males still had their antlers, as they tossed their heads and bawled. Arthur had seen them lose their antlers as early as late January, depending on the weather, so the shed might be soon.

The soft dirt under his feet gave off a whiff of good earth with his every step, and a breeze crackled through the bare trees at the edge of the field.

"Of course you'll win this case," Elizabeth scoffed at him. "Primogeniture has never been successfully challenged. Your parents could have left the bulk of their estate to anyone they wanted, and the eldest son is the usual heir. John doesn't stand a chance." Her Swiss accent sounded like German tones softened with French slurs.

Arthur had known Elizabeth for over a dozen years, but the sibilance of her Swiss accent still disconcerted him. They were in Britain. She should have a polished English accent. When they were in public, her accent remained crisp and British, but she dropped the pretense when they were alone.

She sounded so foreign.

Arthur said, "The courts seem concerned with fairness, lately."

"To hell with fairness," Elizabeth scoffed.

"My barrister is worried about some of John's allegations. He's evidently persuading someone from the National Trust to testify on his behalf."

"Persuade them not to. You haven't been mismanaging your estate too badly, have you?"

"I've put good people in charge of it. I'm rarely here to manage it, personally."

"Blaming me for everything again, are you?" Her voice was light as she teased him.

He raised an eyebrow and one corner of his mouth. "You're a convenient target."

"Good thing our adversaries never agreed with you."

"Indeed. My original barrister died, you know. He was an old hand, knew all the judges and the currents that eddied. My new barrister is pessimistic about my chances. She thinks I'm a waste of a human being. Told me to curtail my 'escapades.'"

"Isn't she sweet." Distaste was evident in Elizabeth's rough voice.

Arthur said, "She is attempting to rein in my activities and contacts."

Elizabeth flipped her hand toward the sunlit trees. "You can't."

"She is adamant."

"So retain a different lawyer."

"A friend in those chambers has mentioned that all the barristers feel the same way. My file was evidently quite the hot potato when the Head Clerk was assigning out Horace Lindsey's cases. No one wanted it, and a new lawyer might insist on my good behavior before taking my case."

"So promise them what they need to hear."

"And then they will remove themselves from the case when I don't follow through."

"I didn't think they could do that. They have a rule about taking cases that are offered, don't they?"

"In theory, but not in practice." His friend had

assured him that the so-called cab rank rule was often discussed but never adhered to, nor enforced.

"So *cultivate* your lawyer," Elizabeth said.

"She's not a Russian mafia princess or a minor sheik. She's merely a London barrister who was given my case."

Elizabeth rolled her eyes, but subtly, just a flick of her eyelids and mascara-darkened eyelashes. She said, "Such sentiment."

"She's an innocent," Arthur mused.

"She's a lawyer. She's hardly innocent. Shakespeare would have had her first against the wall when the revolution came."

"It's unethical."

Elizabeth laughed. "When have we ever concerned ourselves with such luxuries?"

"I won't harm this woman."

"Do you *like* her, Arthur?"

His five seconds were ticking by. Gen's puckish sense of humor amused him. Her intelligence intrigued him. Her lush body aroused him.

He really liked that she hadn't shrunk away from him but had turned around swinging.

His training had saved him from a nut punch or a black eye, barely. She had obviously been attacked, perhaps even abused, and he wanted to stand in front of her to protect her and to wrap himself around her to heal her.

That wasn't like him.

Odd.

Arthur said, "She seems fragile."

"Of course she seems *fragile.* She's not one of us. I'm merely encouraging you to make certain that you win your case. Convince her. You're the best at it."

Arthur looked at the spongy sod beside his shoe. The grass was thin in spots, and the black soil marred the emerald green. "I'm not."

"You learned from the best."

"Certainly." He had been seventeen.

She said, "All my contacts are the highest performers."

"I may have poisoned that well."

"Makes the chase that much more interesting." Elizabeth drew a finger under Arthur's jaw, almost cradling his face in her palm. He wanted to lean into her touch, but he sure as hell didn't.

Elizabeth said, "You're useless to us if you're not the Earl of Severn. Cultivate her so that you get what we need, which is to win your case."

And so, Arthur would cultivate Gen, just like he always did.

Elizabeth withdrew her hand, stroking her fingers under his jaw. "I would hate to lose my best boy."

WHAT COMES NEXT?
STIFF DRINK
(Secret Billionaires #3)

Arthur is enough to make any woman need a stiff drink.

Arthur Finch-Hatten is six-feet and four-inches of ripped, loaded, hot English nobleman who is wasting his life and his inherited estate so audaciously that his younger brother is suing him for control of their family's earldom. There is a darn good chance that Arthur will lose everything, even his crazed, badly behaved puppy.

Genevieve is a lawyer, not a babysitter, and certainly not a dog trainer. She is just about to become a full barrister, a British litigating attorney, when her law mentor dies unexpectedly. She is shuffled off to another barrister, one who's nothing at all like her kind and decent former mentor, and then she is assigned the office's worst case: Arthur.

Get STIFF DRINK wherever you buy books!

Stiff Drink is also available as an audiobook! Look for it where you buy your audiobooks.

A NOTE FROM BLAIR

Hey Folks!

Thank you so much for reading *Working Stiff* and *Hard Work*.

Writing Casimir was so much fun. The big cat in this book that sits in purses is loosely based on my own large cat, who weighs 26 pounds but can wedge himself into a medium-sized purse. When he does this, all his feet are tucked inside, and you can see from the look on his huge, fuzzy, tiger-like head that he is just so pleased with himself.

The rest of the book was fun to write, too, but writing the cats was really too much silliness.

In the next book, Arthur has a badly behaved puppy that you just have to see. I hope you like him.

And Maxence, well, you'll have to see who captured Max's heart.

If you'd like to know when my next books come out, please visit my website or sign up for my email list.

Email List subscribers get lots of free stuff: sneak peeks at works-in-progress, free stories, epilogues to previous books, and notices of new releases and special sales or coupons. Every newsletter has something new, fun, free, or discounted in it, just for you!

Plus, all new subscribers get free ebooks right away!

Please type this link into a browser:
http://bit.ly/BlairBooks

I hope that you'll also leave a review with your thoughts where you bought this ebook. Reviews are the best way to let other readers know about new books or to tell the author that you enjoyed it.

Again, thank you for reading!

Blair Babylon

ALSO BY BLAIR BABYLON

Secret Billionaires Series

Working Stiff ~~~ *Working Stiff* Audiobook

Hard Work ~~~ *Hard Work Audiobook*

Stiff Drink ~~~ *Stiff Drink* Audiobook

Hot Toddy ~~~ *Hot Toddy Audiobook*

Hard Liquor ~~~ *Hard Liquor* Audiobook

Strong Spirits ~~~ *Strong Spirits Audiobook*

Billionaires in Disguise Series (Wulf and Rae)

A Billionaire in Disguise ~~~ *BID Audiobook*

A Tycoon Undercover ~~~ *ATU Audiobook*

A Prince Incognito ~~~ *API Audiobook*

Billionaire Ever After ~~~ *BEA Audiobook*

"An Extravagant Proposal (Charley) Get it FREE HERE."

Billionaires in Disguise: Theo Series

Falling Hard

Playing Rough

Breaking Rules

Burning Bright

Rock Stars in Disguise Series

What A Girl Wants (Rhiannon)

Somebody to Love (Tryp)

The Rock Star's Secret Baby (Cadell)

Santa, Baby (Peyton)

All I Want for Christmas (Epilogue) Get it FREE HERE.

Billionaires in Disguise: Xan Series

"Alwaysland" (Prequel) Get it FREE HERE.

Every Breath You Take

Wild Thing

Lay Your Hands On Me

Nothing Else Matters

"Dream On" and "Keep Dreaming" (Epilogues) Get them FREE HERE.

"Small Miracles" (Epilogue) Get it FREE HERE.

Runaway Princess Series

Once Upon A Time ~~~ OUAT Audiobook

In Shining Armor ~~~ ISA Audiobook

In A Faraway Land ~~~ IAFL Audiobook

At Midnight ~~~ AM Audiobook

Happily Ever After ~~~ HEA Audiobook

Billionaires in Disguise: Maxence Series

One Night in Monaco ~~~ ONIM Audiobook

Rogue ~~~ Rogue Audiobook

Order ~~~ Order Audiobook

Prince ~~~ Prince Audiobook

Royal ~~~ Royal Audiobook

Reign ~~~ Reign Audiobook

Paranormal Romance

Dragons & Magic

Dragons & Mayhem

Dragons & Fire

Check for New Releases by Blair Babylon.

ABOUT BLAIR BABYLON

What order should I read Blair's Books in?
Reading Order
for ALL of Blair Babylon's Books.

More Info about Blair's Books:

Blair's Website: Lots of Fun News, Extras, Reading Order, List of Blair's Books, and More!
www.BlairBabylon.com

Blair's YouTube Channel
free audiobooks and fun author interviews!

ABOUT BLAIR BABYLON

Blair Babylon is an award-winning author who used to publish literary fiction. Because reviews of her mainstream fiction usually included the caveat that there was too much deviant sex in her novels, she decided to abandon all literary pretensions, let her freak flag fly, and write hot, sexy romance novels. She's having much more fun now.

www.ingramcontent.com/pod-product-compliance
Lightning Source LLC
LaVergne TN
LVHW041110080826
845145LV00007B/1748

* 9 7 8 1 9 5 0 2 2 0 3 5 9 *